Per Sempre Means Forever

A Legacy of Love

ROE FASITTA PAGANO

Published by:
Ani and Oliver
Boca Raton, FL
www.aniandoliver.com

Cover design: Jackie Agentis • www.jacqueline@JCAgentisphotography.com
Contributing Photographer: Shelley Arminio • monkeyfacephoto.com
  (female, front cover, and image of Enzo in pregnancy shoot)
Interior design: Gary Rosenberg • www.thebookcouple.com
Editor: Carol Killman Rosenberg • www.carolkillmanrosenberg.com

Printed in the United States of America

To the man who has always been right by my side.
With each and every penny that appears along the way,
I now know that you have never left me and you are
walking right beside me every step of the way.

❧

To the young girl who had the courage to travel the world
to find her true love.
Thank you for being the best mother and friend I could have
hoped for and for allowing me the pleasure of reliving
this incredible journey through your eyes.

Enzo and Laura, I will love you both *per sempre.*

Prologue

South Florida, USA—2008

*T*earful breathing echoed through the house. The sound hitched every now and then in a sob. A weathered photograph of a handsome young couple in wedding attire rested upon a dark, heavy shelf, proudly overlooking the living room. The pair beamed at the camera, standing protectively and defiantly close.

Laura Fellini, her features altered with age, stared at her younger self in the photo. She reached up, took the frame from its shelf, and shuffled away, her shoulders stooped in grief and exhaustion. She was spending her first night alone. The man she had married sixty-one years ago—her beloved Enzo—had passed away that day.

She had chosen to face this night alone. Her two children had pleaded with her to stay the night, but she had insisted they go. At the moment, she wondered if sending them away had been the right choice.

Laura and Enzo Fellini's retirement home in South Florida was a small, but charming, one-story elevation whose exterior reflected the love that existed within its interior walls. The front lawn showed evidence of wear, indicating the place had been lively and active. A few sun-bleached toys stood neatly on its perimeter, waiting to be noticed once again.

Enzo's garden was visible as one approached the house, as it occupied so much of the side and backyard. It had always been a source of pride for Enzo, a symbol of his love for all of God's creations. Bright and beautiful exotic flowers, hearty vegetables, and creeping ivy adorned the exterior walls.

Like his grandfather, Peter, and his father, Giovanni, Enzo had been a man of the earth, embedded deeply with the soil. No one who visited Enzo ever left without one of his extraordinarily fragrant signature gardenias, jasmine sprigs, or roses, their stems wrapped creatively with his signature wet paper towel and handmade tinfoil vase. This was his token gift to all, a little part of himself he chose to share freely and lovingly with others.

A quick sweep through the backyard showed a weathered handmade bocce court, with several balls forgotten midcourt. It looked as if a game had been hurriedly halted. Bocce had been Enzo's game; he had been the reigning champ of the family for years.

The garage stood not far from the backyard. Its inner walls were still adorned with miniature Italian flags and worn canvas maps of Italy, each attached to the walls with faded masking tape. Very old, miniature statues of saints shared and watched over this space. Faded photos of relatives long since departed were scattered throughout. Those photos had kept so many memories alive for Enzo. Pennies were taped to the walls like copper constellations. No one was really sure why they were placed as they were, not even Laura. This space had been Enzo's den, a shrine of sorts to his past.

A weathered workbench sat in the corner of the garage, the resting place for a huge collection of worn tools, garden supplies, and potions for pest extermination. Some of Enzo's own inventions—a frog killer and a can crusher to help him more efficiently recycle—sat there as well. Each new creation carried memories of an abundance of pride and a lot of laughter from his two children and many grandchildren. His inventory—of tools, screws, nuts or bolts, and various supplies for every project imaginable—was well stocked.

Enzo had been known to save everything. "Because," he would say, "you never know when someone might need this." This area clearly served him well; Enzo's collection had been a great resource for all his friends and neighbors. Nothing thrilled him more than finding himself in possession of the one odd tool or gadget everyone was searching for. His eyes would glisten and his signature grin would unfailingly appear.

Enzo had spent hours here, singing and dancing about, creating new gadgets or mending someone's broken something-or-other. This had been his sacred dwelling. He had thrived here. With Enzo gone, the space felt empty. The garden had started to grow out of hand without his meticulous care. And now, too, in the house, where there once had been the incredible smell of homemade sauce simmering in the kitchen as Laura prepared another memorable meal for Enzo and the visitors who stopped by daily, the air was empty. Where once there had been music, there was now empty silence.

A rampant mess of clothing, photographs, medical equipment, and a pharmacy's worth of medications looked out of place in the otherwise tidy home. The disorder seemed to be slowly engulfing the house as Laura wound through a trail of old photo albums, a man's shirt, and long-forgotten mementos.

Laura struggled to accept this new reality. The love of her life was gone. As she anticipated spending the next few nights, the next few weeks, and the rest of her life alone, she felt determined to be strong and to never burden her children. A long-held desire to be independent and take care of herself—on her own—warred with feelings of restlessness, anger, and fear. Intense grief soon won out and she threw herself on their bed, clutching Enzo's pillow and sobbing his name.

When the tears ceased for the moment, she went to his closet, a place she had used for years to store so many of their early, long-treasured belongings, a place she hadn't visited often over the past few years. Her first reach produced their old letterbox. She sat on the closet floor and grabbed a letter from the box. As she lifted the aged, yellowed envelope, a penny fell out onto her lap. Laura peered at the date stamped on its face—1948—and tears streamed down her cheeks. That was the year they were married.

She closed her eyes and pressed the penny to her heart. A multitude of memories overtook her mind. Two days hence she would bury her beloved Enzo.

When she opened her eyes, Laura found herself sitting in a pew in All Saints Catholic Church, garbed in black and surrounded by her children and their families. Her face was distraught, a contrast to the sunny Florida day that passed heedlessly outside, and her hands were shaky. Every seat in this large church was taken, and still more mourners stood at the back of the church.

Laura watched as her daughter, Tessa, stepped toward the podium holding a damp and crumpled letter in her hand, her eyes wet with tears. As Tessa rose stoically at the podium, Laura's throat closed; her daughter spoke as if every word were a struggle.

"My father," Tessa began, her voice quavering. "My dear father . . . how do I talk about my father? I have written a letter to him to help me get through this. I'd like to share it with all of you here . . . Dear Dad . . . "

As Tessa began to read, Laura's mind thrust her back in time, conjuring up images that had gone fuzzy over the years as clearly as if she were living them now. She saw her father, her siblings, and her family. They laughed, cried, thrived, and struggled. She watched babies grow to adulthood all over again. She relived joyous times and difficult times, saw sicknesses long healed replaced with laughter, and those that hadn't . . .

Her strength began to buckle, and her hand closed over the 1948 penny. She clutched it until her knuckles went white. Even as it gave her solace, her heart went out to her daughter, standing teary-eyed and penniless at the podium.

Tessa's eyes remained fixed on the paper. "Dad," she read, "after all I have seen in the last few days, it is quite evident that I did not corner the market on thinking you were such an amazing man. So many saw what I saw, but what I did not know—and I am learning now—is how many people you helped, how many you went out of your way for, and how many you befriended while never expecting anything in return. You were never boastful, but you sure were humble . . ."

Tears prickled Laura's eyes as she saw Tessa's hands begin to shake. Just as Laura began to fear her daughter would crumble, another woman—Tessa's best friend, Lee—appeared beside her. Wordlessly—for words were not needed—Lee took over the reading, never missing a beat, shoulder to shoulder with Laura's determined daughter, who was so much like her father.

"Some could say that you were very complex," Lee read, and Laura noted the quaver in her voice, too, "while others might say you were simple to understand. But I saw how you never forgot any act of kindness given to you. And I saw how you always went out of your way for those that might have been lonely and afraid. I learned the value of honesty and truth from you. I watched you work selflessly your entire life. You were a man who never complained and was always happy to do for his family."

Laura's heart squeezed even as a smile crossed her lips, recalling Enzo's generosity.

"I watched you forgive when forgiveness was unimaginable," Lee read. "I saw you sing and I saw you dance, and no one ever quite danced like you. I saw how you went from a tough man to a softie when it came to Mom and your grandchildren. I saw unconditional love and loyalty in your marriage, and that is a gift that is so rare in today's world. And then I saw you sing again. You were such a happy and grateful man.

"I love that yours and Mom's marriage was such an unbelievable love story. A story that was told throughout my entire life. You never got tired of telling this tale. I love that you were able to love us enough to be tough and firm but to then still be able to express your love to us. I admire how hard you fought to live. I watched you endure unimaginable pain, you fought and fought but never gave up, and I always knew your reasons why. I was always so thankful for this."

Again, Laura felt her mind drifting into the past. She remembered that first long-anticipated sight of Enzo, that first shy kiss that shook the earth. Her first glimpse of Enzo's eyes, staring out from behind the glass face of a picture frame . . . how that picture never did his eyes justice.

"You taught us all the importance of family," Lee continued, "and you fought to have that in your life. You had respect and boundaries and an inspirational relationship with God. You were always loyal to me, and you can rest knowing how much your love and support did for me."

Laura saw Enzo tending his garden. She saw him strive and struggle and succeed, saw even the most stubborn of plants—and the most stubborn of hearts—blossom under his care. She saw him, bright-eyed and smiling, in celebration, surrounded by friends and family. She saw him playing bocce with a fierce competitiveness that never overtook his fierce love for the others playing with him. She saw the tough man who never gave in, but whose gentle nature revealed itself in a deep and abiding love for his family. For her.

Tessa rested her head on Lee's shoulder as she read. Her eyes were streaming with tears. "My promise to you today is that you will be in each of our hearts, every single day. You will never be forgotten. I hope that on your new journey to heaven, you are joined and surrounded by those you love. I know that you will be singing and dancing up there. I hope you are wearing your Mets hat, playing a game of bocce and listening to Frank and Dino. Dad, I love you and always will. Thank you for this beautiful legacy. *Per sempre, your numero uno.*"

Laura saw Tessa reach suddenly into her pocket. She withdrew something small and shining, kissed it, and held it to her heart. Tessa then held the object out in front of her, as if blessing the crowd. Laura's heart leapt into her throat. "I found a penny today, Dad, here in my seat. It was heads up."

There was not a dry eye within the sacred building. Tessa and Lee locked arms as they returned to their seats. Laura knew that for Tessa, it was Lee's presence and enduring friendship that had spanned their lifetime that supported her daughter through these trying months. She had watched the girls' friendship grow since they were five years old and knew what they meant to each other. Lee had allowed Tessa to go through the process of losing her beloved father with complete support and understanding. Lee was Tessa's voice when she could not speak. She knew Tessa would be forever grateful for that. Lee was Tessa's rock.

Laura felt suddenly as if she were looking at her younger self. The penny seemed to hang in the air between her and Tessa. Tessa's eyes, so like her father's, shone with hope. The penny in Laura's hand was warm to her touch.

Thank you, Enzo, Laura silently prayed. *Thank you . . . from both of us.*

As the first strains of the *Ave Maria* began to resound through the church, Laura felt a surge of gratitude for the great love they would forever share.

Chapter One

Partanna, Italy—1943

The bright Italian sun had just begun its descent over the streets of Sicily. Eighteen-year-old Enzo Fellini stood in the mouth of a war-torn alley, watching from the side of the road as a marching column of American soldiers approached. He was neither frightened nor awed, but merely curious. He made eye contact with a passing solider and waved freely to him, a friendly smile lighting up his youthful face. The American soldier smiled in reply and tossed something to him.

Enzo caught the shining object, amused by this exchange. A brilliant American penny sat in his palm. Enzo's eyes gleamed. He held the penny up to the light and studied it well. With a thrill of delight, Enzo saw the date on the penny's copper face was the same as the year of his birth—1925.

This lucky penny will always be with me, he decided. He put it in his sock to keep it safe. He clicked his heels playfully and was off.

Young Enzo was tall and slightly lanky, his body taut with lean muscle. He had a serious, yet welcoming face. He had a logical mind, but he was a deep thinker as well. He was handsome, with eyes a deep green hue that changed with his moods.

Those eyes were full of curiosity now as he approached another group of soldiers. He watched them until they faded into the distance and reluctantly headed in the opposite direction. Moments later, he passed through the bustling main square. It was a grim and tense place, the rumblings of war overshadowing the daily lives of the people who lived there, in war-torn Sicily. Most of them were farmers, sinewy and strong. Enzo waved to everyone he passed, and they returned the gesture with quick smiles.

Enzo approached the doors of a recently rebuilt, somewhat war-weathered movie theater. All signs were in English, and American movies headlined the marquee. Groups of American soldiers milled about outside, and they burst into applause when Enzo came in to view. He flashed his signature smile and waved them off, pulled the keys from his pocket, and proudly unlocked the doors. He swept them open with a flourish and disappeared inside.

The Americans lined up eagerly as Enzo flipped a switch, flooding the doorway with light. This was Enzo's night job. He loved the ease of it and the chance to make a few friends and connect with the American soldiers. But, mostly, he relished what he learned from the movies—a glimpse into the English language and a passion for what was yet to come.

Enzo was highly respected in his little world. He delivered olive oil by day and had a reputation for being an honest, hard-working kid with a strong personal character. He had been studying in college to become a professor when his family had encountered their own health-related struggles that put a burden on them financially. He had immediately altered his plans to help his dad support his family, just as many of his peers had had to do. Everyone in his town found the situation unfortunate and unfair when it came to Enzo; like so many whose lives and plans had been thrown off course by the war, most people felt Enzo's potential had been severely cut short. He'd been on his way to a bright future. Despite his own disappointment, Enzo never complained, embracing his new responsibilities. He took to every new role well. He simply made the best of whatever he had to face.

The American soldiers liked Enzo. Enzo found himself intrigued by them and by America, and he tried to help them out whenever he could. He had just recently finished serving two years in the Italian army himself, and he felt the utmost respect and empathy for the soldiers he encountered. His mother would often provide home-cooked meals to some of them and would do laundry for others. The Fellini family did their utmost to provide comfort and a little piece of home to these men when they could.

When Enzo's shift ended and he returned home, he found a safe and secret storage space for his lucky penny.

Enzo continued to serve faithfully in his duties at the movie theater as the war raged on. Three years of fighting eventually transformed the theater into a hollow specter of its former cheerful self. Few lights worked, windows had been boarded up, and the rage of a fire had left scorch marks on the side of the building. What few lights remained twinkled in the marquee, dim against the waning dusky light. Despite this, many people still came to watch films in the theater. Enzo was still there when the war ended, too, working as hard as he ever had.

Enzo, now twenty-one, kindly encouraged a small group of people to leave the building, mostly poverty-thinned teenagers and a few drunken older men. The years had made him taller and his shoulders broader. He closed and locked the doors behind them, waving goodbye to the last of the crowd and began to make his way home.

Enzo enjoyed the time alone, enjoyed the crushing darkness that was his only companion through the quiet streets of the town. This was his time to be introspective, to feel completely aligned with himself and his thoughts. His feet knew the path well, and he deftly navigated the dips and turns in the road without a need for light.

Suddenly, he rounded a bend in the road and ran smack into a figure lurking in the dark. Enzo stopped, and the man turned around to look at him, his face obscured by a mask. For a moment, neither man moved. In the distance, Enzo could see a partially concealed group of other masked men, guns flashing in the moonlight, looting a nearby shop that happened to belong to a friend of his.

The thug that Enzo had collided with reached out and grabbed him, waving his gun in Enzo's face. Enzo intuitively knew the man was Vincenzo, a fellow around his own age known for engaging in less-than-honorable behavior. As children, these two had been friends, but only for a moment in time, as Vincenzo's character had begun revealing itself early on.

"Say anything and I will kill you," the man snarled.

Enzo stiffened; the voice confirmed his suspicions. He nodded, feeling worried but not scared, more fixated on the store than on himself. Vincenzo's lips curled smugly.

The other men finished their looting and shouted out to Vincenzo. The thug looked at Enzo maliciously. Enzo raised a hand. Too late—Vincenzo dealt him a smashing blow on the side of the head with the butt of the gun.

Enzo's body went limp and he slumped to the ground. The other thugs saw this and hooted and hollered with glee. As the looters began to scatter into the night, Vincenzo called out to Enzo in a voice loud enough to impress his low-class thugs, "Say anything and I will kill you! Remember that!"

Unable to sleep, Enzo rose early the next morning, his head throbbing and a nasty-looking bruise oozing and growing on his temple. He left his home and marched determinedly toward Vincenzo's house. Vincenzo's mother answered his knock. She broke into a huge smile at the sight of Enzo, ushered him inside, and gave him a big hug.

"Enzo, I have some warm brioche and espresso, *mangia, mangia* please!" she cried. "I have some warm biscotti for you to take home to your mother."

He shook his head with disinterest and walked straight to Vincenzo's room, but she thrust a glass of water into his hand anyway.

Suddenly, she saw the wound on his head and cried out, "Oh my God, Enzo, are you okay?! What has happened to you?!"

"Where is Vincenzo?" Enzo replied calmly.

Concerned, she pointed down the hall. Enzo strode down the hall and silently entered Vincenzo's room. The first thing he noticed was the mask, discarded carelessly on the bedroom floor. He stood over the sleeping Vincenzo for a moment, then took the glass of water that stood on the nightstand and poured its contents over the thug's snoring face, followed by the one in his hand.

Vincenzo jolted out of the bed, soaking wet and crazed as he lunged at Enzo, but Enzo leapt easily out of the way. Vincenzo, half-staggered by his sudden transition to wakefulness, straightened his spine and stared daggers at Enzo, water dripping from his chin. Vincenzo was tall, muscular, and frightening all at the same time.

"You're a coward," Enzo said with a scowl.

Vincenzo turned red. "Get out of my house, Enzo," he snarled.

Enzo took a step closer to him. "Don't you ever touch me again. Do you understand?"

Vincenzo shouted back, "Or what?!"

"I'm not here to threaten you," Enzo replied coolly, struggling to maintain his composure. "I am here to simply tell you to leave me— and my friends—alone."

The two men stared at each other for a long moment, neither wanting to be the first to break eye contact. Finally, Vincenzo leaned over and casually lifted his gun from the bedside table. "Have you changed your mind about working for me yet?" he asked conversationally, looking over the weapon as if inspecting it for dirt.

"You know I'm never going to steal olive oil for you," Enzo responded emphatically, "or anything else for that matter."

Vincenzo's face grew red with renewed rage. "I told you, Enzo, you're crazy not to take my deal. Just steal the damn oil. Why are you so afraid? I will pay you nicely."

Enzo stared at him in silence for a moment and then said, "Like last night was any incentive?"

Vincenzo's voice became a low, deadly purr. "Learn this now while you are young," he said authoritatively. "I can teach you all you need to know. Just keep your mouth shut, steal a little oil here and there, and we could both be happier. I just don't understand why you would rather work two jobs than work for me. You have to be crazy to earn a living with your sweat as you do now. I can pay you far better than that Asaro ever could!"

Vincenzo waved a hand at Enzo, at his faded clothing and scuffed shoes, a smile twitching at the corner of his mouth as the gesture encompassed the purpling welt on Enzo's head. He took a step closer, looking Enzo dead in the eye. "This is what you can expect if you don't change your mind," he said, pointing languidly at Enzo's throbbing temple. "You had to leave college to help your family; you gave up everything to make almost nothing when you could be working for me. You could finish your education. You could be rich. You could help your family. How can you not see this is the better choice?"

Enzo's blood came to a near boil. "Vincenzo," he replied, his voice like ice, "I would starve before I would ever work for you. You think this dark life will help you. You will be very sorry one day. Your bosses do not scare me. Don't you ever lay a hand on me again or you will pay dearly. Is that clear? Take this as my one and only warning."

Vincenzo's own eyes went venomous and cold. He raised the gun and mimicked shooting Enzo in the face, but Enzo refused to flinch. He turned impassively on his heel and walked out of the room, down the hall, out of the house, and into the morning sunlight.

Enzo passed Vincenzo's mother in the front yard. She grabbed his arm as he walked past her. Enzo was startled for a moment, and his heart twisted within him as he saw the fear and pain in her eyes.

"Enzo, please pray for him," she pleaded. "Enzo, please!"

She wildly made the sign of the cross, her face streaked with tears. He simply looked at her, nodded and walked away, unable to bear her misery.

She shouted after him, her voice almost a wail. "I am sorry for whatever he has done! Please pray, Enzo!"

Despite her pleas, Enzo felt in the depths of his soul that Vincenzo was a terrible man, much unlike his mother. Right down to his core, he was rotten. But Enzo knew Vincenzo had one weakness, and he knew what it was, but wouldn't play upon it until he knew he really needed to. Enzo would never allow himself to become the kind of man to eagerly exploit weakness, even in the bitterest of his enemies.

But someday, someday.

Enzo was at peace knowing that his time for justice would come. One day, Vincenzo would pay for the wrong he had done. Until then, Enzo planned to be patient.

Enzo returned to his own house, entering as silently as possible and closing the door gingerly behind him. Despite his efforts, the door clicked against the frame as it closed, and his mother, Josephina, came rushing to the door, her eyes wild with pent-up worry. Enzo tried to keep the slightly amused annoyance off his face as she rushed to fetch ice for his bruise and his head.

"Ma, please," he begged, waving her off. "It's fine."

"Enzo, who did this to you?" Josephina demanded.

"Ma, please don't worry about it," Enzo replied.

Josephina made the sign of the cross over his head, muttering prayers intermingled comically with mild Italian curses. Enzo smiled and ducked under her waving hands to kiss her lightly on the cheek.

"Tell me who did this!" she demanded again. "We must go to the police. Dear Lord, tell me! I will kill him with my bare hands. Giovanni, come look at Enzo! Look at what some bastard has done to our son!"

Enzo's father swept into the room and joined Josephina in frantically signing the cross. They prayed in agitated, fast-paced Italian to one hundred and fifty saints all at once—an ability that only they seemed to share and understand.

"Tell me who!" Enzo's mother pleaded, pounding her chest dramatically and fussing with her always-handy rosary beads.

Enzo sidestepped her, exhausted. He looked away and grabbed a letter from the small side table in the entry. He walked through the house toward the backyard, hoping to read his letter in peace.

His mother was still ranting. "Please, just tell me who, Enzo. I bet it was Vincenzo again."

Enzo smirked. "Mama, that will never happen. I can take care of myself. You don't know what we are dealing with here. What are you going to do? Hurt him with your rolling pin?"

Before she could reply, Enzo stepped out onto the back terrace, closing the door behind him. The terrace overlooked the breathtaking countryside beyond. The view of the distant mountains and valleys always gave Enzo pause and sent a thrill of affection rushing through him, no matter how tormented his thoughts became. The fresh breeze coming in from the sea and the scent of fresh flowers filled his senses and soothed his battered soul. It was a magical place, this place he called home.

He sank into a chair and began to read the letter. As he read, he could hear his aunt Teresa's voice in his mind. The mountains in the distance faded from his mind, transforming into the square, soaring skyscrapers of Manhattan.

My dear Enzo,

I already miss the old broken Sicilian sky and the endless fields. It's very crowded here, gray and noisy. A constant buzzing, like birds jumping into the sky. I am blessed to say that I also have a job lined up by my old friend, Caterina, at the coat factory where she works. I feel lighter and healthier than I have in years. My old cough has finally settled down here in America. I am beginning to see that a new beginning for my family may be possible. Enzo, I miss you and I will write you often, my dear nephew. My children wrote me to tell me how well you look after them. I am not surprised. For this, you will always have my love and gratitude. You are like a son to me, my dear Enzo.

Enzo still struggled with the absence of his beloved aunt, who had recently ventured to America in the hopes of making enough money to send back to her family to help her struggling husband and possibly to one day be able to get her family to America.

This had always been Teresa's dream. The American government would only grant permission for one adult per family to come to America to get established. Teresa and her husband agreed that she would be the one who would sacrifice, leaving her children and family behind to make this dream come true.

Teresa had been like a second mother to Enzo, stepping in when Josephina had fallen ill following his birth for a few years. She had cared for the infant Enzo until his mother recovered, and in the process, the pair formed a unique bond that continued to strengthen as the years passed. Their bond was *per sempre*—forever.

Chapter Two

Manhattan, New York—1946

Teresa Zardana stood waiting on the sidewalk, oblivious to the light dancing on the Hudson River behind her. Though slender, she was well built, well dressed, and certainly a bit overwhelmed. She looked out of place on the busy street in the middle of autumn. Several suitcases sat at her side.

The sound of a woman's voice calling her name caused her to turn around. A middle-aged woman with blond hair streaked by slight gray wisps rushed to meet her. She had a brilliant and warm smile on her face. A man came hurrying in her wake. The woman reached for her and embraced Teresa ever so lovingly.

"Caterina?" Teresa breathed.

The woman—Caterina—stepped back, holding Teresa at arm's length, the beginnings of happy tears appearing in the corners of her eyes. The six-year-old girl Teresa barely remembered held no resemblance to this Caterina, a forty-six-year-old woman, except for those stunning blue eyes. Teresa had never forgotten those eyes. Her husband, Vito Baccaro, whom Teresa had never met, embraced her warmly as if they were old friends.

A flood of joy overwhelmed Teresa, and she began to weep, embracing Caterina again. As the two women laughingly parted and wiped their tears, Vito hailed a cab. He stowed Teresa's luggage in the trunk, and all three piled into the car, filling up the backseat.

Moments later, the cab arrived outside Teresa's new apartment on cozy, tree-lined Jefferson Street in Brooklyn. Autumn leaves were strewn about the sidewalk. Caterina and Teresa walked up to the front door of the brownstone while Vito struggled manfully with the suitcases, hauling them up the steps after the ladies. Caterina handed Teresa the keys with a smile, and Teresa unlocked the front door.

"Welcome home," Vito and Caterina said in unison.

The apartment was small and still mostly bare. Teresa had all the necessities to get by thanks to her dear friends. She was blessed and thankful for all the help Caterina provided to make this place feel like a home.

Within weeks, Teresa had adjusted to working and had steadily begun unpacking the few belongings she had arrived with. On a weekly basis, Caterina or one of her family members would come by with food, flowers, or any other items to make the place feel cozy. On most nights when Caterina cooked, she made more than enough to include Teresa. She also brought bags of groceries to her new friend often.

Teresa purchased a few stylish items to decorate her new home with, but her most valued possessions were the photographs of the ones she had left behind in Sicily: her children, her nephew Enzo, her husband, and her extended family. The photos were placed lovingly around her apartment. Teresa was grateful for everything she had and felt her decorating efforts were more than sufficient, as most of her time would be spent at work, making the money her family needed.

Within weeks, Teresa invited the Baccaro family over for dinner to show her appreciation for their support. In the short time they'd known Teresa, the whole Baccaro family had become especially fond of her. The warm welcome Caterina and Vito had extended seemed to be a family trait, one they had passed on to their children.

The small dining room was packed with people. Vito sat at the head of the table with Caterina on one side and Teresa on the other. An unexpected early snowstorm raged outside.

Vito and Caterina's children bustled around, setting the table and bringing food in from the kitchen. Their oldest daughter, Ana, thirty, and her husband, Vic, thirty-one, began serving the food. Laura, fourteen, rushed in with drinks, and Salvatore, six, tried unsuccessfully to sneak bites of food.

Teresa was immediately drawn to the middle child. Petite and pretty, Laura had a happy face, big brown eyes, and beautiful brown hair with sun-kissed highlights.

Everyone finally settled at the table, and Vito raised a glass of wine in a toast. "To Teresa, the newest member of our family. Welcome to America, dear friend."

The clinking of glasses rang in the dining room. Teresa beamed, and Laura smiled shyly at her.

"Pop," Laura said suddenly, turning to her father, "tell her what happened at the store today."

Vito's face flushed with hesitant pleasure, and he obliged, beginning with a flourish and an "Eh, so there I was, minding my own business."

Vito owned a small grocery store called Mr. Jimmy's, located in a three-story brownstone on Central Avenue in Brooklyn. The store occupied the bottom story of their building. Clean, pressed curtains framed the windows of the two upper floors. The brownstone was nestled among a row of buildings that stood overlooking the quaint street. Snowdrifts often lined the sidewalk in winter, during which time Vito and young Salvatore shoveled a neat path every day to allow shoppers into the store.

Within the store, well-stocked wooden crates of vegetables and fruit filled the tiny space. Cans lined the walls, and freshly made pasta hung on racks overhead along with block cheeses, salami, and peperoni. A small counter displayed freshly baked pies, fresh Italian bread, cookies, and other Italian delicacies. Italian soda and a selection of cold-pressed olive oil rounded out the offerings.

The scent throughout was reminiscent of a true Italian market, a tantalizing aroma that wafted out into the street and permeated the air in the apartments above. Vito's standards were high, and the store had an impeccable reputation for the quality of its stock and the excellent flavors of Vito's daily dishes. On any given day the aroma of garlic and onions transcended from the varied plates of fresh sausage and peppers, freshly made meatballs, rice balls, and olive tapenade served with fresh provolone and salami. Here, in his store, he tried to create what he remembered from visiting the marketplaces of Alcamo when he was a child.

Everyone loved shopping there because of Vito. If he was not singing or cooking something for his customers to try, he was joking with guests or shouting suggestions at customers across the store. Vito was kind, fair, and decent to anyone and everyone who entered the store. His heart was, in some ways, his own downfall, however. For those who were facing hard times, Vito couldn't bear to charge. His monthly deficit never seemed to dissipate. He couldn't bear to see anyone go hungry, especially if they had children. He had a huge heart, but he was no pushover; the wiser patrons of the store knew better than to cross him.

The grocery store had been bustling earlier that day. Vito manned the register, a boisterous force among the patrons. Laura's beau, Duke, often pencil–sword fought with Salvatore when he came to visit Laura in the store. That day, Salvatore lunged at Duke, both of them brandishing pencils and goofy grins and perhaps making a bit of a ruckus, but all the regular customers were accustomed to and accepting of it. They all knew Vito's children and had come to expect the sight of one or two of them working there, even young Salvatore.

As Duke and Sal cavorted, an elderly woman entered the store. Vito called for Laura, who poked her head out from the back room. At the sight of her, Duke and Salvatore raced toward Laura, pencils in hand, and began poking her mercilessly with the blunt side.

Laura swatted at her younger brother and smiled at Duke. She broke free and went to help the old woman and carried groceries for her. Duke managed to grab her hand and kissed it as she passed. Laura blushed a fierce scarlet, and the elderly women and Vito shared a knowing glance.

"Mr. Vito, Laura is becoming quite a beauty," said the elderly woman.

Salvatore pretended to barf.

Just then, Mrs. Alagheri—a skinny, harsh-looking woman wearing nice clothing and a mean scowl—entered the store as well. The hard heels of her shoes clattered noisily on the wood floor. She stormed defiantly up to Vito and waved a half-eaten blueberry pie in his face.

Vito greeted her cheerfully, as he did all of his patrons. "Good afternoon, Mrs. Alagheri!"

"Vito, you sold me a bad pie!" she replied shrilly.

Vito looked at the half-eaten pie, and a look of amusement crossed his face. "How are you today, Mrs. Alagheri?" he replied calmly. "Eh, you don't like my pie?"

"No, I do not!" she retorted, her scowl growing fiercer.

Vito's expression became one of amazed confusion. "But you . . . ?" His response trailed off, and he motioned to the half-eaten pie. "You must have liked *half* of it."

Laura, Duke, and Salvatore struggled to suppress their nervous laughter, but a giggle escaped from the younger boy's lips.

Mrs. Alagheri's expression darkened. "Aren't you embarrassed, Vito," she said, glaring at the children, "to have so many children running around in your store? What nuisances they are!"

She'd pressed the wrong button. Vito's calm expression became a scowl. "Eh, listen, Mrs. Alagheri, I'm sorry you didn't like the pie. But you know by now that these are my kids. They go wherever I go. If you don't like them either, that's tough. Next time, bring me the pie *before* you eat half of it, and I'll give you your money back. Or you could make everything easier for both of us and just shop somewhere else."

"No," Mrs. Alagheri snapped. "I want my money back now."

Vito, visibly incensed, responded as calmly as possible, "Eh, Mrs. Alagheri, if you want a different pie, you can buy a different pie."

Mrs. Alagheri boldly thrust the pie under Vito's nose. "You taste it!" she demanded, her voice nearly a shriek. "You taste this pie and tell me it's not undercooked. I'm not paying for bad pie! Give me my money back this instant. And I demand a new pie."

"Well, now we have a problem, eh, Mrs. Alagheri," Vito fired back. "You get this pie out of my face *right now.*"

"Taste the pie!" she shouted, her face as red as a beet. "Taste the pie, you crook!"

Now sweat beaded up on Vito's forehead, one drop running down his face. "You get this pie out of my face now or I will shove it in yours!"

"Mobster!" she railed, her voice becoming hysterical. "You're an Italian mobster!"

With that, Vito snatched the pie out from under his nose and hurled it into Mrs. Alagheri's face. "Now tell me," he said, calmly smirking, "does this half taste any better? It was baked by the same Italian mobster, too!"

Mrs. Alagheri stood riveted to the spot, her eyes wide with shock. After a moment, a blueberry fell from her cheek, hitting the floor with a plop.

Duke, Salvatore, and Laura released their pent-up nervous laughter in heaving, hysterical cackles, nearly falling over one another in their mirth. Mrs. Alagheri's face turned a violent red beneath the purple pie filling, and she began to wail. She raced out of the store, leaving purple splatters in the white snow as she fled, flailing and shrieking, "Police, police! Help!"

Vito mumbled a few expletives in Italian after her before succumbing to laughter himself.

"Well," he crowed as he regained his composure, "I do not think we'll be seeing Mrs. Alagheri again anytime soon, eh? Thank God. Thank God."

By the time Vito finished telling the story, everyone at the table had fallen into helpless laughter, their voices ringing cheerily through the apartment. Teresa herself was holding her stomach, her face bright with glee.

"Oh my God, Vito," she cried, wiping tears of laughter from her face. "What happened next? What did the police do?"

"Eh, for Mrs. Alagheri," said Vito, "not so bad. She went home covered in the best blueberry pie in all of Brooklyn. The police, they do nothing. They love my pie!"

Laughter erupted again. Teresa looked at Laura, who watched her father speak with complete adoration in her eyes. Teresa was falling deeper in love with these good people by the day. It did her heart good to have the noise and laughter to fill her new home.

Teresa noticed how Vito's entire family sat in rapt attention as they watched him tell his story. Soon Teresa would learn that everyone really loved Vito—the whole community adored him. The cops, the customers at the store, and even the criminals had a soft spot for Vito and his grocery store (except, from now on, Mrs. Alagheri, of course).

In the months that followed, Teresa's bond with the family grew by leaps and bounds. She was astounded by the love and support they offered, despite the fact that she and Caterina had been apart for almost forty years. She felt comfortable and confident, overwhelmed by a deep sense of gratitude for her adoptive American family. Teresa now realized that it had to be divine intervention that she had been able to locate Caterina in America after all these years. She was so grateful that Caterina had responded to her letter and was astounded by her willingness to help her in this situation. It was more than she could have ever hoped for.

Teresa and Laura had grown quite close in that time also, and on many evenings, Laura would bring dinner over and the two of them would eat together. Laura seemed comfortable and secure around Teresa and began to confide in the older woman, enjoying a feeling of camaraderie she did not always share with her mother.

It amused and pleased Teresa that when Laura was not with her best friend Jeanne or Duke or working in the store, the young girl chose to spend her time with her. It seemed that Laura had easily made her way into a very special place in Teresa's heart—a place that stood directly beside the space occupied by her nephew Enzo.

Chapter Three

Brooklyn, New York—1946

One night when Teresa was invited to dinner at the Baccaro home, Caterina and Vito caught a glimpse of the tentative hope that was blossoming in Teresa's heart. They had retired to the family's living room after a delightful meal of roasted chicken, salad, and vegetables—with, of course, a second course of homemade lasagna. Vito and his son-in-law, Vic, were engaged in a game of poker. Caterina and Teresa sat together, delighting in the opportunity to chat with each other. Caterina looked up as Laura came in from the kitchen, bearing a pot of coffee and an array of cups on a tray.

"Laura, honey," Caterina instructed, "offer the coffee to your father first."

"She seems like such a good girl, Caterina," Teresa said, her eyes following Laura as she did as she was told.

"Mmm . . ." Caterina mumbled, feeling suddenly uneasy. "I think her father is too easy on her. She has no sense of responsibility. When I was her age—"

"Really?" Teresa interjected. "Do you really want what *we* had for *her?* You really want her to be cleaning up after farm animals at her age? No, Caterina, she is a good girl. She deserves more than we had growing up."

"I learned life lessons the hard way," Caterina replied bitterly. "I can never raise a spoiled daughter."

Caterina—indeed, the whole Baccaro family—had begun to realize that it was easier for Laura to be expressive around Teresa. Caterina confirmed in her own mind that Teresa's arrival in their lives had been a wonderful occurrence and a particularly special thing for Laura. She admitted, however, to feeling a twinge of envy, but only to herself. She loved Laura deeply.

Caterina had also noticed that her friend had been fighting a terrible cough for weeks now, one that seemed to be lingering longer than it should. Teresa had assured her that she felt fine and had refused to go to the doctor or to have a house call. She felt her own remedies would resolve this. Caterina was sure to send Teresa home with some honey for her tea.

Laura made her way around to Teresa and her mother. Teresa accepted the coffee with enthusiastic thanks.

"You're so welcome!" Laura replied, a smile on her lips.

"This is so delicious," Teresa exclaimed. "Don't you think so, Caterina?"

Unsettled by Teresa's demonstrative behavior, Caterina agreed. "Thank you, Laura. It is very good."

Laura's eyes widened at the compliment, and she quickly turned to go, trying unsuccessfully to hide her smile from Caterina. She scampered back into the kitchen. After a few moments, the sound of running water and clattering dishes told Teresa that Laura was washing the dishes. Teresa turned to Caterina again, suddenly very serious.

"I need to thank you, again," she said, holding up a hand before Caterina could protest. "I'm serious. Here I am practically absorbed into your family, by all of your family. We were only brought together for a moment in time as children. Now look at how you look after me. I don't know how I can ever repay you, but you must know this will never be forgotten. I never expected to fall in love with all of you as I have. Thank you from the bottom of my heart."

Caterina felt her heart twist, and tears threatened at the corners of her eyes. "Teresa," she said, clasping her friend's hand, "I have walked in your shoes, and so has Vito. I came to this country alone also, and I know the fear that comes with making such a journey. We all understand what you are trying to do for your family and what it takes to bring them to this country.

"When my parents died, nobody wanted me. I was just six. I want to make sure you never have to feel that way, because I will never forget that feeling. You will never face that fear or ever be alone as long as I am here. Please, no worries about this anymore. This is what we are supposed to do for one another. One day you will help someone in this way and give back to this world. That is what we must all do."

"Caterina, will you tell me your story?" Teresa asked, her curiosity piqued by Caterina's comments. "It's alright if you'd rather not say; I'd just like to know, so I can understand. We only barely knew each other for moment. We were what, six or seven? There is so much I don't know about your life. After your parents died, I know you went from home to home with your elder siblings. I was never able to find you again."

Caterina was not really a talker; she kept her private life private. In this way, she and Vito were very similar. To tell her story—to admit her struggles—was unusual for her. But she felt indescribably close to Teresa and wanted her to understand that her life had not always been what it was today. Still clinging to Teresa's hand, she spoke quietly and earnestly, not wanting the others, especially her children, to overhear.

Caterina began, "When I had first arrived in New York City, the sister with whom I was meant to have lived never came to meet me. Alone, feeling terribly unwanted and scared, I waited for three days in an immigration holding cell before one of my older sisters finally appeared to claim me. She brought me immediately to the coat factory where I have been employed ever since. My sister informed me that her family did not have enough money to feed another person, and so I would need to support myself. I felt so unwanted. They made it very clear that I was a burden to them."

Caterina did as she was told, taking to her new job with staunch determination. Her work ethic was remarkable, and she was well liked in her new environment. She became an adept seamstress very quickly. Despite the chance to make a new life for herself, Caterina was sad. She had lost both of her parents at such a young age, and she felt disconnected, as most of her siblings were much older than she.

On most days, tears glistened on Caterina's pretty face. Her boss's wife, Angelina, noticed her sadness. She befriended her and started to look after her as a mother would. She constantly sang Caterina's praises to her husband, Frank.

One day, Angelina had an idea she hoped would lift Caterina's spirits. "I would like to introduce you to my friend Vito," she told Caterina. "He is a very nice young man. He recently has faced some tough times as well. He has a baby girl named Ana, and I think you all could be good for each other. Just give it some time and think about it. I will arrange it when the time is right."

Caterina was now twenty years old. When she and Vito finally met, instantly Caterina felt as though she found her soul mate and her purpose. She fell in love with Ana, and she saw what a good man Vito was. They were drawn to each other by their own adversity. Initially, Caterina started to help him watch the baby, as he had full custody of her. Soon, he opened up and shared his story with her. Their affection deepened into love. Slowly, they decided to build a life together, and, in time, they married.

As Caterina went on to explain to Teresa, Vito also had his own rough road and tragic path prior to their meeting. Vito's first wife was not the person she had portrayed herself to be during their courtship. They married quickly, but very soon her destructive traits were apparent. She got pregnant almost immediately, and as soon as she did, Vito resolved that he had to be there for this baby, no matter what.

Once his beautiful baby girl was born, he learned the meaning of true love. Ana's birthmother, however, did not. Her drinking seemed to intensify and her habits became very sloppy, neglecting her daughter to visit bars and mingle with men.

One day, Vito had come home from work unexpectedly to check on his daughter, and he'd found her alone in the apartment, awake and uncared for. She had been left completely unsupervised. He was livid. Calling out for his wife and looking frantically for her, a neighbor directed him toward another man's apartment on their floor. When he approached the door, he heard his wife's voice. Without thinking, he abruptly entered. He was distraught to find his drunk wife in bed with another man.

He was heartbroken and humbled. He left that day, taking Ana with him. He knew he could provide a safer environment alone for his child, whom he loved with all his heart.

Not having a lot of family, he called upon his younger brother, Dominick, back in Italy. Dominick himself was unable to come, so he sent his wife, Maria, to help. This seemed an incredible blessing to Vito, for which he was most grateful. Maria arrived within days. Her supervision of Ana allowed him to continue to work and build a new life for himself and his precious daughter. Their future seemed to be brightening.

One day when Vito returned from work, Ana was missing. She had been under Maria's care, and Maria was distraught. She said she had walked Ana to the market to buy fresh vegetables and meat for their dinner and that someone had taken her from the stroller. She had called the police and alerted everyone near. But not Vito. He was not made aware until he came home from work hours later.

Vito was sure that his ex-wife was responsible and felt that she was having Maria followed. Maria was quick to agree and even described instances of strange men following her. Vito searched high and low for days on end, but Ana never turned up anywhere. Not even at his ex-wife's place. It quickly became clear she couldn't take care of her even if she did want her back.

He searched, investigated, worked with the police, and went to work by day. No matter what he did, Vito was unable to locate his beloved daughter. In the meantime, Maria had told him how sad, helpless, and distraught she was, but no longer having a reason to remain, she returned to Italy and her husband. Vito held no grudge against her. He believed she loved Ana and had taken decent care of her. He understood. Vito was left to carry on his search alone. He was now a broken man.

One day Angelina ran into Vito at church where he went to pray daily before work. Vito was alone and desperate. His hands clasped in prayer, he knelt in one of the pews. His eyes were squeezed shut as if, by mere force of will, he could bring his baby back. Angelina, unaware of what had happened, as they were just fairly new acquaintances, was more than a little alarmed by his demeanor. She knew Maria a bit better than Vito because they shopped at the same market. Angelina was always quite taken by baby Ana. That is what had brought the two women together.

"Vito," Angelina asked, looking around for Ana's stroller, "where is your beautiful baby and Maria?"

Vito froze, then burst into tears, pouring out the whole story and opening up his broken heart. Angelina sat by his side, stricken with horror over his story. She felt terrible for Vito. His pain was palpable.

A few weeks after this encounter, a sudden realization struck Angelina. She could not get Vito and this story out of her mind. She remembered she had heard Frank, her husband, talking to someone about a missing baby. She hadn't connected that this could be Vito's daughter he had been speaking of. Not wanting to get his hopes up, she said nothing of this to Vito.

Frank was a good man and very connected, a fact that both served him well and gave him a formidable reputation. He owned the coat factory and many other legitimate businesses, in addition to a few side businesses that were not quite so legitimate. He knew all the right people in all the right places. Sometimes—very, very rarely—he did the wrong thing.

Angelina worked tirelessly to keep him on solid ground. She loved him dearly, and she spent a lot of time in church praying for his soul. Angelina immediately went to Frank the very same night this thought appeared and asked him what he knew of this situation.

"Frank," Angelina pleaded, "Vito is a good man, and we have to help him. He is suffering so."

Frank did many less-than-honorable things, but children were simply off limits. Angelina knew this. Frank confessed to her that he had heard someone from another "family" was involved in taking a baby, possibly to Italy. Frank had firmly disagreed with this and had voiced his opinion when asked. Nevertheless, the deed was done. Frank knew he couldn't control the world, so he'd let it go.

"Who, why?" Angelina asked. "What family has done this? You have to find this baby! She's such a beautiful baby girl."

So, in an act of deference he only ever showed to his wife, Frank did what he was asked to do. He asked around, utilizing his connections, and learned everything he could. Someone had definitely been paid to kidnap little Ana and bring her to Italy.

As soon as the truth came to light, Angelina called Vito immediately and asked him to come to the coat factory. She led him into the office so they could speak privately. Frank came in to the room and, with a calm expression that belied the seriousness of what he was about to say, told Vito that the conversation was never to be repeated.

The information he shared brought Vito to his knees. He exclaimed he did not have money to take a trip to Italy; he did not know if what Frank said was even true. Frank assured him it was accurate information. Vito left, his heart heavy, to plan his next move.

A few days later, Angelina again summoned Vito to the coat factory. Frank walked into the small office and said, "Listen, Vito, we know where she is, we know who hired and ordered this, and I have a guy who is willing to go there to get her back."

Vito's mouth fell open in shock. "Who, why, how much?" he demanded. "Go, yes. I will work for the rest of my life to find this bastard and kill that son of a bitch. If it is the last thing I will ever do, I am going to kill him. I vow to you."

"Vito," Frank said, laying a placating hand on Vito's shoulder, "it was your sister-in-law, Maria. She paid Carlo Valenti five thousand dollars to kidnap Ana and bring her to Italy. She has been raising Ana as her adopted daughter with your brother. Your brother, Dominick, believes the baby was abandoned at a hospital when her unwed mother died giving birth. She had the nurses deliver the baby to Dominick while she was here, believing it would appear more credible. That's the story she's going with."

Vito was torn between relief for himself, rage toward Maria, and pity for his brother.

"Carlo is willing to help get her back to us. . . ."

Vito's head shot up, peering eagerly into Frank's somber face.

Frank paused before continuing. "For ten thousand dollars."

Vito's face grew ashen. His hands began to shake, and he dropped his head into them, his shoulders heaving, and wept aloud. "Why, dear God, why?"

Frank straightened, his mouth a grim but determined line. "Vito," he said, "we *will* get Ana back for you."

Vito froze. Slowly, he lifted his head, meeting Frank's firm gaze with his own confused one. "How?" he asked, and then added, "I will simply call my brother and tell him the truth. He will return her to me."

Frank quickly replied, "Vito, no! You will never get her out of the country legally. You would be arrested immediately. This Maria has people expecting you there. You need to stay away and let me handle it."

"But I don't have that kind of money," Vito said, hanging his head.

"Leave it to me and trust me. Don't ever think of stepping foot in Italy, now or in the future. Trust me, Vito," was all the reply Frank chose to give.

Within three weeks, baby Ana was back with her father, and there was never a more grateful man on the face of the earth. She had been gone for four months. Frank and Angelina had chosen to lay out the money so that Vito could have his baby back.

When Vito had expressed his grateful disbelief, Frank had shrugged and told him, "You can pay us back in time."

Within the first few weeks of Ana's safe return, Vito trekked to the coat factory to bring the first installment of his repayment. Frank called him into the office. When Vito tried to hand him the money, Frank pressed it back into his hand.

"Thank you, Vito," he said sincerely, "for doing the right thing. You showed up, you delivered, it is done, and it is over. I will never take a nickel from you. Go and live a good life with your daughter.

That is an order. Someday, you will do something nice for a deserving soul. God will put in them in your path. Your job is to go make a difference."

Vito embraced his benefactor, silent tears of joy streaming down his face. Frank released him, patted him on the back and gestured for the door, his eyes twinkling merrily. Angelina embraced him as well, kissing him soundly on the cheek.

Frank smacked him lightly and playfully on his cheek and said, "Vito, go. Get out of here, go."

Vito grasped his hand, thanked him, and turned to leave. As he was about to step out of the office, Angelina called for him to wait. "Vito," she said, gesturing to a stack of fabric in the corner, "would you mind bringing this heavy bolt of fabric over to that young blond girl sitting out in front for me? My back is killing me."

Vito obliged, grabbing the bolt of fabric as he made his exit. At the door, he quickly turned around and said, "Frank, how much to destroy my sister-in-law?"

Frank and Angelia immediately jumped up. "Vito, no," urged Frank. "We got her. She is yours, and she is unharmed. Never look back. Let it go. Living with that will kill you. God will take care of this."

Vito now knew he could never go home, never see his brother again. He realized if he saw Maria, he would kill her with his bare hands. He could never forgive the insane act she had committed.

Frank said, "Go, Vito, get out of here. Go love your baby girl."

Angelina added, "Please, Vito, just drop this bolt of fabric off to my girl for me. I really have too much pain to lift it. The blonde over there. Go, go, go!"

That girl was Caterina. Vito walked on air as he left the coat factory, thinking of Caterina's pretty face and ocean-blue eyes.

Frank and Angelina were attentive and involved in Ana's life going forward. In a sense, they became her godparents. Angelina and Frank never again brought up the money or what they had done for Vito or Ana.

Frank owned a majority of the territory that occupied the area of Brooklyn surrounding the factory. Vito's grocery store would eventually open in this area. One day, not long after Caterina and Vito were married, Angelina and Frank saw Caterina crying at her workstation in the coat factory.

"The boy's from Ralphie Rizzio's family were in yesterday," Caterina tearfully confessed to Angelina. "They threatened Vito unless he pays up. They say they want a piece of our business and that we have no choice in the matter. They want so much. We just don't have that kind of money."

Frank immediately called Caterina into his office to hear the whole story. After this, the threats and demands for payment ceased; Vito was off limits. Forever. Vito never did anything dishonorable to earn this protection, nor did Frank ever ask for anything in return for it. The two men simply shared a mutual respect. Vito felt eternally indebted to Frank and Angelina. How blessed he was to have them in his life, as he knew he was incapable of ever returning a favor equal to what they had done for him. To this current day, they never made him feel that they wanted or expected a thing. It was unconditional.

Vito had food delivered to the factory every day in abundance. If food is love, in Vito's mind, this was his way of showing them what was eternally in his heart. And every day, they relished the gourmet delights that arrived at the factory like clockwork at 12:00 PM sharp.

Catherina went on to explain to Teresa that she and Vito were eventually blessed to have more children. "They were both little boys who suffered untimely deaths. Both were named Vito. The first was a beautiful baby boy lost at birth. We were devastated. In time, we were thrilled to give birth to another little boy. In the first one's honor, we passed on his name to the second. At ten months, both he and Ana came down with influenza. When the doctor came for a house visit, he had inadvertently injected Ana's dose of vaccine into the baby and his into her. Ana recovered, but baby Vito died shortly thereafter. My Vito suffered greatly over this loss. It took him years to recover. The loss of his two sons was more than he could handle . . . Me, I suffered, mourned, and persevered. I put it in God's hands."

Teresa reached out and gently stroked Caterina's moist cheek.

Caterina smiled sweetly at the gesture and continued, "Laura came along eventually and then, years later, another boy. We could not name him Vito. Salvatore, our shining star, was finally here. He has two sisters who are much older than him. Do you think he feels like he has three mothers and may be a bit indulged?"

Teresa chuckled.

"Life has not always been easy for us, Teresa. But it has always had a good outcome. We have stuck together, and we made a family. Vito's children are his life. He still has not resolved what Maria did, the loss of never going back to Italy or ever confronting his brother with the truth or seeing his brother again. This is such a sore subject. He refuses to talk about it. But we thank God every day for what we have."

"Thank you for feeling safe enough to tell me all of this," Teresa said, once it was clear that Caterina had said all she had to say. She fell silent for a moment. "I am sorry for all your loss, grief, and pain. This story is devastating. My heart aches for you both."

Again wiping a tear from Caterina's cheek, she paused and then said, "I am the one, aren't I? The one Frank said you'd have a chance to help?" She chuckled, and then added, "The *deserving soul?* I am so lucky that I have you making a difference in my life. Frank and Angelina helped you and now you're helping me. I am honored to call you friends."

"For whatever Frank is, Teresa," Caterina replied, "know he has a good heart. Angelina has been such a blessing in our lives."

Teresa suddenly realized that it was Frank and Angelina's affection for the Baccaros that had landed her the job at the coat factory. Every blessing that had come into her life since she'd arrived in the United States led back to the Baccaro family. They all were so kind to her; they had even given her an extra warm coat once winter set in.

"I promise to do the same one day, Caterina," Teresa said firmly. "I promise to do for someone what you all have done for me. I don't know what I would do without you."

Caterina patted her hand, raising her voice so Vito could hear,

"We look forward to the day the rest of your family can join us here. We cannot wait to meet and embrace each and every one of them." Caterina knew in heart that Teresa was a special soul and an amazing, kind, and unusual person. She was a rare gift and her goodness stood out. Caterina was glad to have this woman back in her life.

Vito looked up with a smile, and Teresa shifted uncomfortably in her chair. "My daughters, maybe," she replied, "but it is my nephew, whom I love like a son, I wish could come here. But he could never—would never—leave his family. I really want the chance to make a difference in his life. I want him to enjoy the freedoms of America, as much as I want it for my own children."

Vito asked, "Why is that?"

"He is the most upright and noble young man I have ever met," Teresa said, a wistful smile blooming on her face. "He is my brother, Giovanni's, oldest son. He had to leave college to help out at home. He works two jobs now to help support his family. He helps look after my family, too. I took care of him when he was a baby. He is like a son to me. He is so good that it breaks my heart." Teresa shifted in her chair, squaring her shoulders with pride. "In fact, I just received a letter from him, and he told me the most disturbing story about a local thug named Vincenzo who wanted him to steal from and dishonor his current employer. When Enzo refused, Vincenzo beat him to try to make an example of him. Enzo is not afraid to do the right thing."

Caterina and Vito murmured in admiration.

"I just worry, because his heart is so good. I just want him to be safe. He worries about me and he writes me almost daily. He wants to make sure that I'm safe. He felt terrible that I was leaving Italy."

The noise in the kitchen suddenly ceased, and Laura returned to join the family. Hoping she was not going too far, Teresa looked first at Vito, then at Caterina.

"I hope you don't mind," she said, suddenly feeling the need to be completely honest, "but I have written to all my family and shared all I can about your wonderful family. Ana's beauty, Salvatore's spunkiness and, of course, all about Laura. I see something special in her. I know it may sound crazy, but . . . some of the rare qualities I see in

Enzo, I also see in Laura. She reminds me of him. I see the two of them . . ."

Caterina seemed to grow nervous and openly did the sign of the cross, a flash of defensiveness crossing her face. "My God, Teresa," she said with a laugh, "he sounds wonderful, but Laura is only fourteen. You are lucky to have him, and I will pray for his safety."

"Yes," Vito growled, "she is my baby girl who has a long way to go yet." He cast a look of concern toward his wife. Abruptly, he turned back to the card game, scowling and muttering under his breath in broken English, "Eh, crazy in the head! She is only fourteen. She is a baby!"

Laura frowned at Vito in confusion.

Salvatore popped up from his place on the couch. "Ma," he crowed, giving Laura a cheeky wink, "you know she already has a boyfriend! I saw Duke kiss her and I saw her kiss him back!"

Laura gaped at him in shock. Her face went crimson, and she leapt at him, chasing him around the room. She caught him easily, threw him onto the couch, and began to tickle him.

"I'm sorry, Juliet!" Salvatore cried, gasping for breath between giggles. "Give me ten dollars and I'll take it back."

"Enough!" Vito bellowed, pounding his fist on the table, sending playing card leaping into the air. "All this talk of kissing is giving me indigestion! Laura, go get me the *brioschi*. You better not be kissing anyone!"

Teresa suppressed a smile as Vito leaned back in his chair, his face red, and rolled his eyes exasperatedly up to the ceiling.

"Ay-ay-ay," he sighed. "I will have to kill anyone that goes near you, Lulu. The *brioschi,* Laura, bring it quickly."

Laura winked at her father and scuttled out of the room, sticking her tongue out playfully at the little brother she adored as she passed him.

Chapter Four

*E*nzo looked up from reading his latest letter from Teresa as his father, Giovanni, stepped out onto the terrace. Enzo straightened up, sitting stiffly in his father's commanding presence.

Giovanni took a seat, reached into his pocket, and withdrew his tobacco pouch to refill his distinguished pipe. He spent a moment packing the bowl, then produced a match from his other pocket, struck it on his boot, and lit the pipe. Then he motioned to the letter in Enzo's hand, the unique scent of his tobacco permeating the air around them.

"What did she say?" Giovanni asked with a puff on his pipe. The pipe always seemed to linger on his lips when he had a lot to contemplate.

"She said not to worry about her," Enzo replied, looking down at the letter as if searching for a specific line to avoid meeting his father's stern eye. "The Bacarros are taking good care of her. She is so grateful to have found them. The husband, Vito, is originally from Alcamo, but Caterina, his wife, is from here. Her family originated from Partanna. Teresa knew her briefly as a child. Do you remember her, Pa?"

Giovanni scowled and gave a curt shake of his head, crossing his arms over his chest.

"She says she's feeling well," Enzo continued, trying to reassure him, "and that she likes America. She misses everyone. I hope to see America one day, too."

Giovanni sighed, pulled the pipe from his lips, ran a hand over his face, and shook his head at Enzo. "She shouldn't have gone," he said, his voice firm and sad. "I can't imagine just leaving my entire family as she has! She belongs here with us. Not with those strangers." He gave Enzo a pleading, accusatory look. "You could have stopped her, Enzo. She listens to you more than anyone else. My baby sister belongs here with us, to be with her children. Not across the ocean. She could have sent her husband."

Giovanni rose angrily from his chair and turned away, glaring at the distant mountains. His head tilted until he was looking upward, and he shook his open hands in a posture of prayer, as if he were pleading silently with the heavens. After a moment, he dropped his hands, spun on his heel, and stalked back toward the door, cursing Teresa's husband for letting her leave.

Enzo raised his voice to call after him, "Pa, you couldn't have kept her here."

Giovanni froze in the doorway, his shoulders raised defensively. He turned his head slowly and leveled a glare at Enzo over his shoulder. "You could have, Enzo, only you," he said. He turned and walked into the house.

Enzo watched the door swing shut. Surprising himself, he noted he didn't feel any guilt for not trying to stop Teresa from taking her journey. Somehow, her actions had felt right to him, just as they had to her.

The door of Teresa's Brooklyn apartment swung open, and Laura hastened in. An unexpected spring storm raged outside; rain and snow smacked threateningly against the apartment window. She shimmied out of her coat, depositing a pie on the kitchen counter and newspapers on the coffee table before hurrying to where Teresa sat, writing at her small desk.

Teresa accepted Laura's delicate kiss on the cheek with a smile, watching her as she moved around the apartment. The space was much cozier now, full of comfortable furniture, bright rugs, and soft pillows. A new letter from Enzo sat on Teresa's desk, begging to be read.

Laura bustled back to the kitchen. "Mom sent me over with a pie," she said cheerfully, cutting a slice as Teresa rose from her desk and made her way to the dining room table, her eyes twinkling with amusement at Laura's fussiness.

Teresa took the slice Laura offered and winked. "Mmm," she said, giving it an appreciative sniff, "Blueberry!"

Laughing, Laura offered her hand to help Teresa into her chair. "Your hands are so soft, Teresa," she said. *But so thin,* she thought with a tinge of worry.

With a conspiratorial tone, Teresa told Laura that the secret to soft skin was olive oil lotion. "My sister-in-law makes it," she said. "Would you like some? I have an extra bottle."

Laura reluctantly declined, but Teresa wouldn't take no for an answer. "Nonsense!" she replied with a wave of her hand. "There, on my desk!"

Smiling, Laura hurried to Teresa's desk. As she lifted the bottle of lotion, her eyes fell on the photo frame beside it. A young man smiled out from behind the glass. Laura lost herself in his eyes for a moment . . . brilliant, sparkling eyes that she fancied were either green or blue.

Teresa cleared her throat, and Laura flushed instantaneously. Teresa laughed and motioned for her to bring the picture over. Laura obliged, sinking into the chair next to Teresa and staring at the handsome face in the photograph. Teresa ate her piece of pie slowly, trying not to grin too broadly at the dreamy look on Laura's face.

"He's handsome," Laura breathed.

"He is my nephew," Teresa confessed. "His name is Enzo. He sent me this new photo last week."

"That's Enzo?! I never imagined. He looks like a movie star!"

"Yes, Laura, that's what I think. He is one in a million."

Laura's reaction to Enzo's photo seemed to amuse Teresa, but Laura was startled by the physical reaction she felt just from looking at his photo close up. She had never experienced a sensation like this. It seemed impossible to remove the smile that had spread across her face. She was hypnotized by Enzo's eyes and his smile, frozen in time behind the pane of the picture frame.

Teresa watched Laura's face with a pleased, humorous smile. Had Laura been able to drag her eyes away from Enzo's face long enough, she would have seen the soft glow of contentment and peace shining from Teresa's eyes.

Teresa had not missed the look of concern that had flashed in Laura's eyes when she had taken Teresa's thinned hand. Her cough—an insidious thing that came from deep within her chest— had begun to show signs of overtaking her body. She was sure Caterina had given Laura specific instructions today to report back to Caterina on her health. She suspected that her childhood friend thought she was hiding the severity of her condition . . . and perhaps she was. She had openly refused to go to the doctor, afraid of what might be discovered. She chose to keep denying to herself and the Baccaro family that it was anything serious. She needed to put all her attention on laying a foundation here in America for her family.

She subconsciously pushed the thought of her health out of her head, and when Laura left the apartment that day, she sat for a moment and reflected on her feelings for this lovely young girl. Laura had a caring heart and a zest for life. In fact, she embodied all that she loved in her own three daughters; she was certain her girls would love Laura, should they have the chance to meet as she hoped they would.

Teresa deeply valued the time she and Laura shared one on one. She found joy and fulfillment in helping Laura perfect her Italian. But even more so, she felt incredibly blessed to be the one with whom Laura freely shared her dreams and desires. She knew Caterina was somewhat envious of this closeness, but she also knew her friend trusted and valued Teresa's newfound role in Laura's life. This was never a conflict.

Her mind flashed back to Laura's eyes as she'd studied Enzo's face in the photograph. *If that's how she felt just seeing his picture* . . . The thought nagged at her mind and refused to go away. *Enzo and Laura*, she thought again, and a smile came over her face.

Right then and there, Teresa decided she would take matters into her own hands. She knew what she hoped for was improbable, but not impossible. She had felt this from the day she met Laura. Returning to her desk, she sat down to write a letter to her nephew. The pen scratched quietly on the paper, the only sound in the apartment to accompany the pattering of snow on the window.

> *Dear Enzo,*
>
> *The Baccaro family continues to be so giving and loving. The food is abundant, delicious, healthy, and fragrant! In the kitchen something magical is always being prepared. It reminds me of ours back home before the war. Their lives are full of music, laughter, noise, and family. To see such joy and love does my heart so much good. I am able to forget my longing for my own family, even if it is just momentarily.*
>
> *I have been more than blessed to have found them, but today I write about their beautiful daughter, Laura, who reminds me so much of you! It is my relationship with her that intrigues me the most. I am fortunate to have her trust. She shares her innermost thoughts with me, which fill me with such hope and inspiration. But my mind keeps bringing me to you, my dear Enzo, whenever I am with her. When I look at her, I see your eyes, I see your smile. It is my desire that one day . . . I see destiny.*

Teresa's hand faltered as a fit of coughing overtook her. Unable to continue, she rose from the desk and staggered to the bed, barely reaching it before her strength gave out. Even as she struggled, her thoughts dwelt on Laura and Enzo. *I must bring them together one day.*

Laura had just turned fifteen, and Enzo was about to be twenty-two. However, Laura was no ordinary fifteen-year-old girl. She was mature beyond her years. They were oceans apart. But something in Teresa's heart told her that what she was trying to accomplish was the right thing to do.

The next morning, Laura stopped by Teresa's apartment on her way to school. She told Teresa the purpose of the visit was to see how she was feeling, but Teresa suspected she wanted to get another close up of Enzo's picture. When Teresa caught her scanning the apartment for Enzo's picture, Laura turned beet red, grinning from ear to ear. It was not where it had been the day before.

Teresa handed it to her, and Laura let out a sigh. "Oh, he looks like Cary Grant," she said.

Teresa laughed and ushered her out, hiding the fact that she felt worse than she had the day before. She decided to finish the letter, and before sealing it, she suddenly decided to drop in a photograph of Laura.

❦

A couple weeks later, Teresa's letter awaited Enzo in the front hall of his home. He tore it open enthusiastically and pulled the letter from the envelope, looking forward to reading Teresa's continuing tale of her life in America. As the letter came loose from the envelope, something fell out and floated to the ground.

Enzo looked down where the mysterious paper had landed. It was a photograph. Of a girl. No, an angel. A beautiful angel. He reached down, holding his breath, and gingerly scooped up the photograph. Who was she? Why had Teresa enclosed this photograph?

He looked back at the letter. Perhaps his aunt would tell him all about this mysterious beauty. He walked dreamily to his favorite spot in the garden, not once taking his eyes off the young woman in the photograph. And even as he read the letter, he kept the photo pressed against the paper with his thumb so he could glance at it every so often.

❦

Whenever Laura visited with Teresa now, she would ask all sorts of questions about Enzo. Teresa had not let on to Laura that she had sent the photograph or mentioned any word of what she had in mind for the young couple. Nevertheless, the pair shared guarded banter about Laura's fascination with the young Italian man. Laura tried hard not to be transparent, but Teresa was very astute when it came to matters of the heart.

As the weeks passed, Teresa noted that Laura's Italian had improved immensely, as had Teresa's English. Happily, Teresa's health seemed to be improving as well, not by much but enough to offer some hope.

Caterina and Vito seemed a bit taken aback that their daughter had taken such an interest in Italy and her Italian culture of late. Her questions of Teresa never eased up. She didn't speak much of Enzo in front of her parents, keeping her blossoming obsession with the mysterious Italian to herself. She was fighting an internal struggle with her reaction to this new situation and that picture. She could not get that face out of her mind.

When it came to her curiosity about Enzo, she even tried to be guarded with Teresa, at times. The older women was too perceptive not to have an inkling of Laura's deepest thoughts when it came to her nephew, and, truth be told, Laura wasn't very adept at hiding her true feelings from her. In any event, Teresa firmly believed that knowing more about Italy was Laura's birthright, and she shared everything she could.

One day when the family and Teresa were gathered around the Baccaro table and Italy was the topic of conversation, Laura asked Vito, "When can we visit your hometown, Papa?"

Caterina eyes widened, and Vito said, "We are here in America, Laura. Italy is a fond, old memory. We will not be going back."

"Why not?" asked Salvatore, not understanding the silence demanded by his father's grave tone.

The head of the Baccaro household stood up from the table. "I have my reasons."

The rest of the family understood not to pry any further, but Laura's interest in learning more about Italy did not falter. From then on, Laura stored up her questions for the next time she and Teresa would have some time alone.

Laura knew her fascination with Italy was a direct result of her fascination with Enzo. Of course, she couldn't allow herself to believe that this was more than just a schoolgirl fantasy. Duke smothered all of her free time, and she liked him just fine. He was handsome in his boyish way, and she knew he was smitten with her. He was her sure thing. But there was no intrigue there. As more time passed, the more she found herself enjoying her private fantasy. And the less she found herself wanting to hang around with Duke.

As had become her habit, Laura would stop by Teresa's mailbox to retrieve the mail, always hoping there would be a letter from Italy. It had been a few weeks now since she'd become enthralled by Enzo's photograph, and no letters had arrived in the interim. Today, though, she had a strong feeling Teresa would hear from her nephew, but she didn't dare sort through the mail. She handed the small assortment of envelopes over to Teresa when she went inside.

Teresa shuffled through the few letters and then looked up at Laura with a smile.

"This letter is for you, Laura," she said.

Laura reached out an unsteady hand to take the letter from Teresa. She instinctively knew it was from Enzo even before she read the return address. She took the letter in her hands and felt a jolt of energy pass through her palms. He, her Italian mystery man, had touched this very envelope, and now she was touching it, too. It was almost as if they were touching each other. She started to shake.

She passed the letter back to Teresa. "Here, please open it," she said, her voice quivering.

Teresa quickly opened the letter, careful not to unnecessarily tear the envelope. She slowly pulled out her nephew's letter and handed it back to Laura, anticipation written in her expression.

Laura unfolded the sheet of paper and looked down at the beautiful penmanship. She quickly scanned the words, discovering she couldn't read a word—at least not in her present state. "It's in Italian," she told Teresa, as if she were shocked.

Teresa chuckled. "I'll read it to you, Laura. Sit, sit down, and listen," she coaxed.

A jumble of nerves, Laura did as she was told and looked over at Enzo's photograph. He had written to her. *Her* Enzo had taken the time to share something with her. She kept her gaze on Enzo as Teresa began, reading one line at a time in Italian, then pausing to allow Laura the time to translate his words in her mind.

Dear Laura:

It is my pleasure to meet you. Although we have not formally met, I feel like I already know so much about you. On behalf of myself, Teresa's family, and her very protective older brother, my father, Giovanni, we are all indebted for the love and care you all have given to this wonderful lady. She boasts of the time you and she get to spend together. Thank you for filling in for her family while she endures this life changing sacrifice for her children. One day it is my wish to meet and thank you and your family in person. You see, I am in awe of America. It is a huge desire of mine to venture to your country.

I work in a movie theater by night as a projectionist. It is an American theater, mostly for the benefit of the wonderful American soldiers serving in Sicily. I am honored to be around these fine men. But it is what I see on the screen. It is what I hear on that screen. It is all about a most intriguing place and interesting place. It fills my senses and leaves me hungry, filled with so much curiosity about the vast differences of these two countries . . .

When Laura returned home that evening, she tucked Enzo's letter in the back of her top dresser drawer. Then, full of unfamiliar emotions, she retrieved her stationery set from her desk, took out a pen, and began to write.

Dear Enzo:

I am happy to meet you as well. Teresa has shared so much about you. She certainly has a deep love and respect for you . . .

❦

And so it began—the frequent exchange of words, ideas, desires, histories, and dreams for the future. Their letters to each other crossed the Atlantic, time and time again. The anticipation of those letters elevated Laura and Enzo's emotions to levels neither had ever known.

While Laura wouldn't allow herself to fully believe that Enzo was more than just a pen pal, she still kept this exchange from her parents and everyone else, except for Teresa. She would get the letter from Teresa when one arrived and bring it home, where she kept it hidden in her top drawer along with the others. It became Laura's nightly ritual to wait until everyone had gone to bed, then she would double check the hallway once more to be sure no one was lurking about, and then spread all of the letters out on her bed. If she had a new one to read, she would start with that one. Then, she would reread the others.

Early on, she had stopped asking Teresa to translate. She knew enough Italian now to be able to translate for herself, and Teresa had been more than willing to take herself out of the equation. This was proceeding exactly as the older woman had hoped.

As time passed, Laura and Enzo moved beyond the formalities, such as Enzo's appreciation of her and her family's warmth toward Teresa, and all the basics such as family background. They compared notes on American movies, which Laura would see months before they would reach Enzo's theater in Italy. Laura made a game of sending Enzo her favorite lines from the movies, and Enzo would listen for them from his projection booth and send her those same lines back in Italian.

They also wrote to each other about what it was like to live in their respective countries and their hopes to someday experience each other's world for themselves. Enzo told Laura all he knew about the world from where he sat, and she told him what little she knew. She wrote about her father's store, and he told her about his work at the theater and selling olive oil. She talked about school, and he told her that someday he hoped to go back to college.

On and on this went, until Laura began detecting somewhat of a more amorous tone in Enzo's letters, which both excited and frightened her. Her "pen pal" had begun to conclude each letter thusly: *Per sempre, Enzo.*

Every single one.

Chapter Five

Enzo parked his pickup in front of the outdoor marketplace and unloaded the heavy jugs of olive oil to be delivered to several stores and a few restaurants on his daily route. He thought about Laura momentarily, and he realized they had been communicating for almost a year. He had one of her letters tucked in his back pocket, which he had read at the post office and would read again at his next opportunity.

He entered a small shop where a tall, slender girl stood behind the counter, looking sleepy and bored. He whistled a low whistle, causing her to perk up immediately. She picked up a muffin and hurled it at his head, scattering crumbs everywhere. Enzo tried to catch it and ended up crushing it, festooning the front of his shirt with more crumbs.

The girl laughed and leaned over the counter to clean off his shoulder, the touch lingering longer than required. She smiled that familiar Sophia Milazzo smile at him. He playfully glared at her and snatched a loaf of bread from beside her. Baked goods were abundant in this quaint area of the market, and Enzo was clearly comfortable there.

"Hey, you have to pay me for that!" she shouted.

"One day, Sophia, I promise!" he replied with a wink as he walked away.

Sophia smiled and watched him unblinkingly as he left.

After the oil had been delivered, Enzo approached the theater to begin his shift, carrying Sophia's bread and a fresh block of Parmigiano-Reggiano cheese. He already had his stash of his favorite Asaro olive oil in the projection room.

As he unlocked the doors, he slipped inside and headed to the projection booth. A movie was already underway. Reels of film adorned every available space in the small room. To Julian, his coworker, Enzo's appearance meant his shift was over. Julian gave him a loose hug and said, "See you later, Enzo."

Alone now, Enzo watched the movie playing in the theater below him. He munched on the cheese and dipped the bread in the golden oil. He mouthed the words along with the actors. He pretended to laugh when the characters laughed and pantomimed their movements. When he had had his fill of bread and cheese, and with the movie rolling for at least another half hour, he took out Laura's letter and read it again. Then it was time for him to write. What else could he do? This American girl was all he ever seemed to think about.

Dear Laura,

There are times when I am sitting in the dark of the booth, listening to the rhythmic whirring of the film, as I watch the careless dust swimming in front of the stream of light. I think about how all those stolen kisses appear on the screen and in the stream of light in front of me. How they can appear so beautiful.

Yet unknown to the crowd just feet below me, I am held captive in this room to be so still, yet, have the ability to have my mind wander and travel just as easily as the speck of dust in front of me. My thoughts take me to America, to you . . .

Laura sat in her crowded schoolroom at P.S. 162. Oblivious to her surroundings and the rambunctious students stirring around her, she didn't even hear her teacher trying to regain order. That Duke was drawing images on her back from the desk behind hers was inconsequential. She only had eyes for Enzo's letter snuggled between her textbook pages. She imagined him sitting there in the projection booth writing to her of dust and travel. His letter went on to describe the sunflowers that grew along the mountainside in his Sicilian garden. His words carried her away to another place, and she felt like she was floating.

Suddenly her imagination took her to his projection booth where she was sitting by his side in silence. She imagined him reaching out to touch her hand. In doing so, his hand became illuminated. Then suddenly hers was as well. A great movie—an epic tale of love—began to play in miniature on their youthful skin. She envisioned a light flash across his face, further illuminating his eyes. The light intensified and Laura pulled back; his touch frightened her so.

Laura's best friend, Jeanne, knew about Laura's Italian *pen pal,* but Laura had kept the details vague. When Jeanne would press her, Laura would say it was nothing. Lately, though, like right now, Jeanne could tell something was up with her friend. They had been best friends all their lives and knew each other like the backs of their hands. Laura had been becoming increasingly more distant and somewhat tense. Today, Jeanne decided Laura was going to need to come clean.

She caught Laura's attention from the seat beside her. "Meet me in the bathroom after class," she said. "We need to talk."

Laura obediently followed Jeanne's orders. Her friend hadn't left her much choice by the tone in her voice.

Once in the bathroom, Jeanne demanded, "Laura, tell me what is going on with you. I know you. I know you better. Duke sees it. I see it. You are a million miles away. Tell me. Can I help?"

Laura's eyes welled up. She glanced down at the white tiles on the floor and then back at her friend. "I wanted so badly to tell you, Jeanne. But . . . oh, I don't know. I thought if I spoke it aloud, it would all go away. But it is becoming so real."

With a wave of relief, Laura filled Jeanne in on how her *pen pal* had become so much more over the course of the past year. "I knew I could trust you with this," Laura assured her, "but I didn't trust myself to speak any of it out loud. Not with anyone."

She went on to tell Jeanne how it had all started so innocently and that she had been entirely truthful with herself in the beginning, but now, she told her how the messages had intensified in the past few months.

Jeanne was happy to have cracked the code, but still she was shocked that this Italian man had grown so fond of her friend. "This is such an incredible love story! Oh my God, it's like a movie!" Jeanne was a hopeless romantic.

Laura let a wide smile emerge. "It is, isn't it?"

"I want to know everything!" Jeanne said. "Do you have a picture of him?"

Without hesitation, Laura produced Enzo's picture, and Jeanne gave a cry of delight. "He *is* a movie star! Those eyes! He looks exactly like Cary Grant. Oh my God!"

Laura was thankful to have her best friend's support. She'd felt guilty not sharing this blossoming romance with her. That weekend, the girls spent countless hours in Laura's room looking over Enzo's letters, dreaming of an improbable future and giggling while they plotted possible scenarios involving this amazingly romantic and handsome Italian. Together, the girls relished in the splendor of what could be.

"What does this mean?" Jeanne asked, pointing to the bottom of one of the more recent letters. "*Per sempre?*"

"It means forever," Laura replied.

A knowing glance passed between the best friends. Laura's face became flush, and no words were spoken. No words needed to be spoken. Jeanne knew in her heart how real this was—possibly even before Laura herself could admit it.

When Laura next visited Teresa, the pair exchanged small talk for a bit. She hadn't spoken much of Enzo to Teresa once they had begun exchanging letters on a regular basis. She kept the mention of him to a safe level, only mentioning details that were pertinent to what was going on in Italy, but Teresa already knew those things, as Enzo had continued to write to his aunt faithfully as well.

But now Laura had a burning question to ask. "Teresa, may I ask you something?"

The frail woman reached out her hand to Laura, who took it gingerly with both of hers. It pained Laura to see Teresa's condition worsen off and on, and right now, it seemed to have worsened.

"Of course, Laura, my love. Tell me, what is on your mind?" Teresa asked.

Very hesitantly, Laura began, "Enzo signs all of his letters with the words *per sempre.*"

Teresa nodded.

"Why does he do that? How can he know this is forever? It confuses me so much. I don't know what to feel," Laura said all in one breath.

Teresa grasped Laura's hands tighter and brought them up to her lips for a kiss and then held them to her heart for a long moment. When she released them, she made the sign of the cross. "Talk to God," she told her. "Trust in God and never stop. He knows what he is doing, so never forget these words. That is all you need to know to get through any doubt. *Per sempre.*"

Laura trusted those words with all her heart. She trusted Teresa. She smiled to herself, thinking of that wonderful phrase: *per sempre.*

Teresa then told Laura, "I have something that I'm very excited about to share with you today. I just got word that all the papers have cleared for my three daughters to come live with me here in America. I know they will love you and your family. They feel as though they already know you because I have shared so much about you with them."

Laura was thrilled for Teresa. Everybody was. Everyone knew how much she missed her family. Within weeks, Teresa's three daughters would arrive in the United States, and it would be as if Bacarros were welcoming family they had known for years. Teresa's three daughters would prove to be stunning and just as warm and wonderful as Teresa on the inside. They would all bond quickly.

But for now, Teresa had a quiet moment to reflect, her thoughts settling on the divine intervention that seemed to be at play in all of their lives. She still marveled at how meeting this one family had supplied her with all she needed in making this drastic change in her life. Maybe this was also God's way of bringing two beautiful, young people together: Enzo and Laura.

❦

That night, Laura took the time to respond to the latest letter from Enzo, debating if she should be as revealing as Enzo had been. As Laura watched her words form on the page, she feared she was in so deep that she could never return to the life she once knew without Enzo in it.

> *Dear Enzo,*
>
> *New York is not black or white, but it is not Technicolor, either. The city can be awash with soot, sometimes making the whole place both muted and ever changing. I, too, see the dust particles you mention floating in front of my eyes that you see in front of your projection camera. And when I do, I see what you see. I see your garden, your mountains, and the beauty of your Sicilian countryside. Those tiny specs of dust become the magic that transports me to where you are. I live in the words you write to me and I feel, smell, and see all the images and flavors you have shared with me.*
>
> *This has never happened to me. Your words seduce my whole being, it seems. I am just a girl . . .*

When Laura reread her letter before sealing it, even she was floored by the words that had come so easily to her. She was starting to acknowledge all the possibilities opening up to her.

As Enzo sauntered through the marketplace, he heard Laura's voice. His surroundings transformed in his mind, the air becoming hazier and brownstones lining the streets. He walked along with phantom crowds of fast-paced New Yorkers, buzzing with a thousand conversations. Suddenly, the crowd enveloped him until he became unrecognizable. The crowd surged and morphed, and then Laura emerged. He reached out his hand, and she took it in hers.

Shaking the daydream away, Enzo suddenly realized he had crossed an emotional line. He was now living in Laura's world. How could he return to the life he once knew without her in it? Why should he?

Now that Laura's secret was out, Jeanne could not contain her excitement over Laura's long-distance romance. On a daily basis, she confronted her friend with her overwhelming enthusiasm. She hounded her with requests to read his newest letter, to hear Laura's thoughts on the topic, and to see his pictures again and again (Laura had amassed a small collection). The girls decided he looked most handsome in the one in his army uniform, but truly he looked handsome in all of them.

At times, Laura was amused by Jeanne's voyeuristic interest in the "love story" and so pleased to have a close friend with whom to celebrate this secret. Today, they laughed as Jeanne asked, "Do you think he has a friend for me?"

At times, however, this banter would frighten her, as these feelings were so new and foreign to her.

If you could view the distant lives of Laura and Enzo from a higher perspective, you would see two vivid imaginations working tirelessly in a futile effort to bring them physically closer. You would see two young people, each sitting alone in a movie theater oceans apart, because there, in the theater, they could somehow feel connected. You would see them mimicking the actors' actions, playing their roles, mouthing the words, throwing their heads back in laughter, and wiping away tears over lost love and painful goodbyes.

You would see the angst of a young man and young woman, each anxiously awaiting his or her next letter. But mostly, you would see simultaneous smiles appearing on two beautiful faces as they read each other's words. You would see an inexplicable longing on their faces and in their eyes to gaze upon each other in the flesh. Each would be caught off guard as a floating speck of dust sparkled in the light of the projector, offering so many dreams and possibilities.

Chapter Six

*L*aura cautiously entered Teresa's New York brownstone, shortly after Teresa's daughters had left for school. When she had knocked, she hadn't heard Teresa's usual greeting to enter. At first, the scene in front of her did not register; it was too horrible to believe. Her eyes opened wider, and there was no denying it: Teresa lay sprawled on the floor, blood on her mouth and splatters on the rug. She was coughing uncontrollably.

"Oh, my God! Teresa!" she shouted, running to her friend's side.

Teresa caught her breath and managed a whisper. "I am very ill. Get help. Then go tell your *father* . . . not your mother, to meet me at the hospital."

Despite her panic, Laura gathered her strength to call for help. It seemed like an eternity before the paramedics arrived, but in reality, it was just a few minutes.

As Teresa was being lifted onto a stretcher, she weakly told Laura again to get her father.

A brief moment of silence passed, and then Laura pounded down the stairs and ran out of the brownstone. Her pale face was distorted by terror. She hesitated on the stoop before determining which way to run. She ran in the direction of her father's shop.

Vito was manning the register. He had heard the faint shouts in the distance, which were somewhat muffled by the siren of an ambulance. Clearly now, though, he heard Laura crying, "Pop, Papa, Pop!"

Vito met Laura on the sidewalk. Snow flurries fell into their hair and melted. He tried to console his hysterical daughter, while at the same time he struggled to understand what had happened to make her so distraught. Laura pulled away from his embrace, shaking her head furiously. And that's when Vito went rigid. He suddenly understood without any words between them. He turned and sprinted toward Teresa's apartment.

Laura watched him go, trying to determine where she should head next. She made her decision and took off in the opposite direction.

Laura raced through the coat factory, past rows of sewing machines and miles of fabric. She turned a corner and saw her mother. She hesitated, soaked in the buzz of the factory, and tried to regain some semblance of composure.

Caterina looked up and saw her, shooting her a brief look of surprise and then turned her attention back to the sewing machine. "Laura, what are you doing here? You should be at school," Caterina said without looking up.

"Mama, I—"

Caterina interrupted, "I don't know why your father doesn't encourage you to get to school on time."

"Mama," she began again, "it's Teresa. Papa went to her. You need to go to the store. To wait for his call."

The stricken look that crossed Caterina's features pained Laura deep within. She watched her mother transform into a small, unsure version of herself. Caterina made the sign of the cross, and then clutched her rosary beads, which she always kept hidden somewhere on her body. Her lips moved in prayer.

At that moment, Caterina's supervisor peeked around the corner, giving each of them a concerned glare as he cleared his throat. Laura looked back at her mother, sensing that Caterina would be unable to hold it together.

"Mama, go. I'll do it. I'll finish it. Go," she offered.

Caterina repaid Laura with a swift look of gratitude, and Laura felt a guilty moment of pleasure to have this connection with her mother. She watched Caterina sprint down the corridor, before turning her attention to the coat. She suddenly felt very overwhelmed.

Vito arrived at St. Mary's Hospital, a sprawling building that looked somewhat out of place in Brooklyn. When he entered Teresa's room, she seemed comfortable enough lying in the hospital bed, but he noted with alarm how shriveled and depleted she looked. Like Teresa, Vito had chosen to ignore the warning signs leading up to this day and had shaken away Caterina's concerns over the past year.

He took a seat beside the bed and took Teresa's frail hand in his own, much larger one. He had already spoken with the doctor. The prognosis wasn't good. Likely, Teresa had advanced cancer of the lungs, and maybe even the stomach. Maybe even elsewhere in her body. She had waited too long to get help.

Vito tried to remain composed, but his words came out in sobs, "Teresa, Teresa, oh my God, Teresa. . . I am here."

Teresa suffered a momentary but violent coughing fit, then gasped for breath. She tried to offer a weak smile, but she was fading fast, as if she were trying to remain awake following a sleepless night. She motioned for him to come closer and whispered into his ear.

"Thank you to you and your family for all you have done for me. I love you like my own. You have filled my time in America with great joy and love. I thought this sickness would pass. I had too many dreams and work that had to be done. . . . Your Laura made my days so happy. I love your girl, Vito. There is a letter for her in my apartment. Be sure she gets it when she is no longer grieving. Tell

Caterina I have loved her like a sister. Tell them both I will take all the good they have done for me straight to God—"

Vito tried to interrupt, to somehow convince her—and himself—that she would make it through this, but he knew it was futile. Teresa weakly waved away anything he might say.

"Vito, you must make me a promise," she implored, gathering her last remnants of strength for this important conversation.

"Anything for you, Teresa," he said with all sincerity, blinking away the tears in his eyes.

"Take Laura to meet Enzo in Italy. This is my dying wish. This is why God brought me here to this place, to your family. I know in my heart that this is what must happen. I will not rest in peace until you make me this promise."

Vito had never expected such a request. "Enzo? Your nephew?"

Teresa's slight chuckle turned into a cough, and Vito stood until she was able to catch her breath. He shook his head, dumbfounded, and paced a few feet back and forth along her bedside.

"Vito, please. I beg of you. They have been writing to each other for over a year now. They have developed a close bond. You need to take her to Partanna to meet him."

"To Partanna? No, Teresa," he said quietly, sitting back down beside her. "What you're asking me is impossible. My family's home is in Alcamo. Partanna is too close. I can't risk it."

"Vito, times have changed."

"Not for my family, they haven't," Vito insisted. "My sister-in-law, she is still crazy. And I hold secrets from my brother."

"It's been thirty years. How do you know? Caterina tells me you haven't seen your brother in all this time. Take her, Vito, to meet her family . . . and my Enzo."

Vito ran a hand through his thinning hair. "I would love to see Dominick, but he's married to that vile woman."

Teresa argued, "Despite your personal struggles, these are your issues. Laura she needs to know her family. She needs to meet Enzo."

"Teresa—"

"Don't deprive Laura of her birthright, Vito. Don't you want her

to see the beauty of the old country? The wind, the ocean, the sprawling sky? It's part of her. It's all a part of her. Enzo is part of her now."

Vito wasn't fully grasping the significance of Teresa's insistence
that Enzo and Laura have a chance to meet, as he was too distraught
over the thought of returning to his hometown. "I *can't* go back."

"If Laura where my daughter—"

"She isn't," Vito interrupted. "She is mine and Caterina's."

There was a stunned and painful pause.

"You're asking the impossible," he said apologetically.

"Maybe," she responded, "but trust in God. He has a plan."

"You have no idea what this would mean," Vito responded.

Teresa's eyes suddenly cleared and their laser focus pierced his
own. "I make this request of you, and you alone, Vito, because I know
your heart understands mine." It went unspoken that Caterina would
not be so understanding.

Vito struggled internally, sensing something greater than himself pulling at him. He walked over to the window and looked down
at the city streets. How could he not honor a dying woman's final
request? He returned to Teresa's side and took her hand again. "For
you, and you alone, I will do this. Go in peace knowing your wish will
be fulfilled."

He kissed her pale cheek. He saw the suffering on his friend's
face and felt riddled with guilt that he could be so selfish at such a
moment.

Teresa squeezed his hand, smiled, and closed her eyes. The mon-
itor at her bedside sounded an alert, and a nurse came rushing in. A
flurry of activity followed, and Vito was ushered from the room.

❧

Enzo rushed to the front room in response to the painful bellow
that had erupted from his father. He found Giovanni openly weep-
ing in angry despair, while Josephina unsuccessfully tried to console
him. Enzo spied the neatly torn telegram with U.S. postage. His heart
dropped.

Giovanni screamed, "My sister! My beautiful little sister!" This was followed by an inhuman-sounding howl, and Josephina shrank back.

Enzo sank along the wall in speechless despair. He briefly thought of Laura and felt a slight twinge of jealousy that, of the two of them, she had been the one to enjoy Teresa's last year of life. This was quickly replaced by a desire to console his young American friend, for surely, she was suffering as much as he was. They would suffer together in their own way—oceans apart. The bustling cityscape in his mind suddenly appeared empty, the concrete buildings devoid of life. This image echoed how he felt inside.

Laura stood nervously in the sanctuary of St. Joseph's Catholic Church in Brooklyn beside Teresa's open casket, her eyes red-rimmed from crying. She pulled Enzo's final letter to Teresa from her pocket as well as one she had written to Teresa upon learning of her death. Her lips quivered as she kissed the letters and tucked them alongside Teresa's lifeless body. This was her last goodbye to someone she had genuinely grown to love, someone whose friendship had changed her life. She vowed to never forget her.

Laura had never before experienced the death of someone close to her. The pain of saying goodbye to this wonderful woman felt almost crippling.

She turned as Teresa's three daughters entered the church, striking and all dressed in mourning black. They clung to each other, their grief becoming more dramatic as they neared the casket. Laura felt horrible for them. They were the only immediate family members who had been able to attend. It was by the grace of God that they got to spend the last remaining months with their mom.

Laura had hoped that Enzo would come, but she knew he worked hard for what little his family had. She could only imagine the pain he was feeling and wished they could share their mutual grief in person. She glanced over at Duke with appreciation. She was happy to have his support, especially since she had been so distant from him for the past several months. She knew that he knew this was not the place to try to win back her affection. Nevertheless, she went to his side as Teresa's daughters paid their last respects. The three young women were devastated and heartbroken.

The hysteria of their grief touched Laura so deeply that it tore at her young heart. After a few minutes, one of Teresa's daughters had to be escorted out of the church to restore order to the sanctuary. When another tried to lift Teresa's body out of the coffin, Laura fainted.

When Laura shuffled into the kitchen a few months following Teresa's demise, Vito and Caterina froze mid-argument. Laura felt weary and cold. The colorful Italian landscape in her mind had become scorched fields. The letters to and from Enzo had all but ceased, as both were grieving; they somehow shared an unspoken belief that they shouldn't carry on as they had been now that Teresa was gone.

Laura felt older now, at sixteen, taller and more womanly than she had been when she had first met Teresa. Yet, she also felt like a child who had no concept of how to deal with death or the disturbing images that remained in her mind. She shuffled to the sink, poured herself some water, and shuffled out again.

Caterina shook her head.

"She's taking this too hard, Vito. That scene at the church would have made even the hardened cry," Caterina said, her voice filled with motherly concern.

Vito nodded. It was a hard day to forget, even for them.

Caterina resumed their argument, "To me, she's still a little girl. She's still a baby. Travel to Italy to meet a young man? It is absurd. But how would you even do this? You would close the store for the summer?"

Vito responded, "No. I was hoping you would take over?"

"Are you asking me to give up my job so you can take a vacation?" Caterina asked incredulously.

Vito countered, "It will be a sacrifice for all of us. You know this won't be easy for me. I'm not running out on you. I made this promise. I must honor my word. Teresa deserves this respect."

Caterina sighed deeply. "I need you here, but I know in my heart you must go see Dominick and give Teresa the peace she so deserves by taking Laura to meet this mysterious nephew of hers." Caterina knew it was time for Vito to make peace with his brother. It had gone on for too long.

"This was never about us. This is about Teresa and our broken daughter," Vito reaffirmed.

Caterina exclaimed, "I'm heartbroken, too! Teresa became like a sister to me. She meant more to me than my own flesh-and-blood sisters!"

"I know. I know, my love," he acknowledged. He pulled her into a hug, and she buried her face in his chest.

Finally, they had come to an agreement to honor the promise Vito had made to Teresa.

⚜

Laura lay on her bed, facedown. Caterina stood awkwardly in the middle of the room, looking around as if she had never seen it before. Hand drawings, small photos, various pieces of mail and art were tacked to the wall. The room was colorful and cozy, and Caterina wondered at all of it. She was nostalgic for her little girl and the loss of the best mutual friend she and her daughter would ever share.

Caterina lowered herself onto the bed slowly, and Laura sat up. She reached over to hug her mother, feeling glad to have her close despite the distance in their relationship. Caterina stiffened initially, but then softened.

Laura swallowed hard. "I still miss her, Mama."

Caterina exhaled and quietly began to sob. Laura stroked her hair, as Caterina had hers when she was a little girl. It never ceased to amaze her how unsure of herself her mother would become when her feelings were exposed.

Caterina composed herself after a moment, and peered at her daughter. "I hear . . . I hear you've been writing letters?" she said.

Laura's face flushed instantly, and Caterina bit back a smile. Laura nodded, sheepishly went to her stash and pulled out a stack for Caterina's reaction. Caterina's eyes grew as she examined the impressive collection.

"Teresa translated all of these?" she asked.

"Yes, in the beginning, but I practiced, and after a while, I could read them on my own. She even taught me to write in Italian, but Enzo—that's his name—understands a lot of English words, so I would write most of my letters that way."

Caterina looked at her and then back at the letters, shaking her head. "Well, Teresa certainly had something up her sleeve, didn't she?"

Laura handed her mother the framed picture of Enzo, which she had collected from Teresa's apartment shortly after her death. Caterina looked at the handsome young man with appreciation. "You have to meet him, don't you?" she said.

Laura's eyes widened. Caterina's eyes instantly filled with tears. She gazed at her daughter with pride, already feeling lonely for her presence.

"Meet him?" Laura asked, disbelieving but hopeful.

Enzo sat in his room. He drew a thin letter out of an envelope. He turned it over in his hands before he read it, his curiosity piqued by the unknown handwriting. He read it quickly. His face grew flush. He read the letter again just to be sure. A wide smile stretched across his face.

He ran through the house to the kitchen and surprised Josephina with a hug. His mother spun around, startled by the sudden affectionate embrace. He held the letter out to her.

"She's coming, Mama."

Josephina read the letter. Then she clapped and laughed.

Enzo beamed. He took the letter and called out, "Pa! I have just received the most incredible news!" With that, he took off toward the back garden. "She's coming!"

The Fellini home had been a somber one since Teresa's passing. As Josephina turned back to the stove and stirred her sauce, she expressed thanks to God that the time had come for joy to return to their household. And that joy would be in the form of the young American woman Teresa had spoken so fondly of.

Josephina smelled magic in the air, mingling with the aroma of bubbling roasted tomatoes.

◈❖◈

Enzo careened into the square at Partanna market, bursting with energy. He marched up to Sophia's store and grabbed a small pastry. She laughed as he ate with gusto.

"Laura is coming to visit!" he said between bites.

"Who?" Sophia asked.

"The American girl I've been writing to."

"She's flying here from New York?" she asked incredulously, her temperature rising.

"She's flying here from New York!" Enzo responded enthusiastically.

Sophia snickered at him and shooed him away. "Get out of here. You're scaring away my customers."

Enzo looked over his shoulder at her and said, "I can't wait for you to meet her, Soph." In a singsong voice, he added, "You're going to love her."

In the same singsong voice, Sophia said, "I doubt it," but Enzo did not hear her. She stuck her tongue out at his retreating back as he traipsed happily and obliviously through the market.

Chapter Seven

*L*aura stared at her reflection in her bedroom mirror. She held a piece of paper in her hand. She studied the paper and took a breath. She stared at herself again, looking away from the paper.

She garbled the speech she was trying to memorize: *"Ciao. Il mio* name . . . *nome . . . è Laura. Il piacere è tutto mio. . . . è incontrarti. . . .* Italy, er, *L'Italia è* very . . . *bello. Sono* . . . darn it! *Sono . . . felice di essere qui."*

She wrinkled her nose at herself in the mirror and gave up. Reading and writing Italian was one thing; speaking it was another.

"I am terrible at this," she said to Ana.

Her older sister placed a hand on her shoulder, gazing lovingly at Laura's reflection. "You will be magnificent!" Ana assured her, thrilled that her sister would be taking this trip.

Ana's approval meant the world to Laura. Ana was beautiful; her clothes, her skin, her hair were always impeccable. Laura looked up to her big sister. Her mind had been running in so many directions. She was excited, but she was also scared. She was grateful to have Ana's support.

"Ana, do you have any advice? What will happen in Italy? Do you think Enzo will like me? Will I like him?" Her questions went on and on as she modeled her new clothes before packing them into her suitcase.

Ana finally held up her hand. Her older sister said simply, "Laura, I love you. But you must listen to your heart. Always listen to your own heart."

So, the next day, Laura did just that. When Laura said goodbye to Duke, she could tell he knew she wasn't just saying goodbye for now; she was saying goodbye to the possibilities for continuing their relationship upon her return.

"I must follow my heart," she told him. "It's telling me to take this trip, Duke, and it's also telling me that there's someone special out there for you."

Duke only nodded forlornly in response.

When she said goodbye to Jeanne, she told her friend she would carry her with her in her heart always.

"Go take Italy by storm!" Jeanne encouraged. "And then get back here to report it all!"

The girls laughed.

Laura ruffled her brother's bushy hair, and then settled into her mother's embrace for a long time. They had grown closer during this time of their shared grief, and as she prepared for the trip, Laura appreciated their newfound friendship.

She and her father got into the taxicab following their tearful goodbyes and headed to the airport. They remained mostly silent, each lost in their thoughts about what awaited them in Italy. Before long, Laura found herself on an airplane. The sights and sounds were all new to her, and she greeted them cautiously but with great excitement. As she prepared to take the window seat her father had directed her to, she spied a shiny penny on the cushion. She picked it up, thought about her good fortune, and settled in for the long flight. She watched a crewman scurry around outside the window and shivered with anticipation.

Vito smiled at her, and she tucked the penny into her pocket for luck.

Days earlier, Enzo and Josephina had taken the train out of Partanna to the airport in Rome. Enzo had watched his hometown dwindle into the background. The people in his town were excited for him to be meeting the American girl. Many of his friends had even gathered at the train station to bid him farewell. He had tucked Laura's picture into his wallet, with a penny taped to the back of it for luck.

The next day, Enzo stood at the airport, clutching a bouquet of wildflowers, wearing his finest suit, and bouncing with nervous energy.

But Laura did not show up.

The next day he went back. He wore the same outfit and carried a new bouquet.

Still no Laura.

The following day he waited again, flowers in hand. Again, Laura failed to arrive.

"You must have received the wrong flight information," Josephina assured him when he began to lose hope. "*No one* has come from America these past few days. We must wait another day."

Enzo hoped his mother was right. Growing increasingly despondent, he decided he would wait one more day. He honestly did not know how he could go home without Laura. If she turned out to be a no-show, he would just have to join the foreign legion, he decided. There was *no* other way to save face. As for his heart, there would be no saving that.

⟨Ⴤ⟩

After three days of travel, the plane finally began its descent. Vito snored loudly in Laura's ear. Despite her own exhaustion, Laura was wide awake. It had been a trying ordeal for both of them. The 24-hour flight had made several stops to refuel, and all food was prepared and consumed at the terminals they visited. She had had no idea what a long journey this would be. A million scenarios had occupied her thoughts to ward off the boredom. But now, Laura's face came to life as the plane emerged from the clouds and revealed expansive, beautiful, lush Italy. She gasped audibly, rousing Vito, who peered over her shoulder sleepily.

For the last three days, he had spent uninterrupted quality time with his daughter. He was so proud of who she was, the heart and sense of self that she possessed. Vito felt he had done his job well and that there was nothing more he could expect from his beautiful daughter.

They had talked in depth about this experience, Teresa, her loss, what it meant, and Enzo. Why he had never wanted to return to his homeland never came up. Vito felt that some things were better left unsaid.

They had talked about Teresa's dying request, which both had found enlightening on so many levels. Vito had decided this trip was the right time to deliver Teresa's letter to Laura. Laura had been so thrilled to receive it, and especially on the plane flying over Italy. Laura told her father that she thought his timing was perfect. She had called it a precious gift and said that it was almost as if Teresa's spirit was traveling with them.

When she had opened the envelope, she felt melancholy upon seeing the handwriting she had come to know so well. She almost felt she could hear Teresa's soft, sweet voice once again.

Dear Laura,

When you read this, my darling girl, I will be gone. I know you will take my loss hard. But what is most important is what you do with what we had. How you carry the bond that we created. I ask that you carry it with you every day. What you do with the love we created and what we felt toward each other is most important. Remember that this is a beautiful thing and this will never, ever disappear. We will always have this. The trust, the life lessons, and now your relationship with me and God must go on forever.

A piece of me lives within you now and I put my faith in knowing that you, along with my children and Enzo, will live for me a little bit every day. That is all I can ask.

Please don't question why I never spoke of my illness. It took over and won. I tried with all I had, but my resources were limited. God called me home. I will forever be that shining star that will be watching over you.

Because of your family, Laura, I was never alone in America. Because of YOU, Laura, I WAS NEVER LONELY. You will never know the sheer joy your company gave me. I loved that you felt safe enough with me to share your thoughts and secrets and I was so thrilled that you felt safe enough with me to dream of things that could still be possible in your young world. You may know by now that it is my wish that you and Enzo meet one day. I see things beyond your years, my sweet child, and what I see in you and Enzo is surely meant to be. I know you feel something and I know the core of who you two are, in your souls, is only something God could create. I am only the messenger.

Remember when I am gone to always turn to God for your answers, for your comfort. He is always there and always listening. One day, remember when you think of me and you need me, I will be that shining star looking upon you. Always near. Please go forward with no sadness; sing and dance and always be that Laura that I fell in love with the moment I met your sweet face.

Laura, I will never forget how you took care of me and looked over me as if I was your own Mother. My family and I will be forever indebted to you. Please live a beautiful life for you and for me.

My love Per Sempre,
Teresa

With each tear Laura had shed as she read Teresa's words, she felt that a pain was being lifted from her heart. This letter connected to her heartstrings, and the agony of loss was being released. She felt empowered, connected, and ready to face all that was about to cross her path once she stepped off the plane. She whispered out loud, "I love you, Teresa, forever. Thank you."

When Laura finished reading, Vito had grabbed her hand,

squeezed it, and said, "She loved you, Laura. I have done my part. Now it is up to you to do as she asks. She will always be alive in your heart."

Father and daughter had fallen silent then, and their trip continued with a beautiful understanding between them.

Now, as the plane was about to land, Laura said, "Welcome home, Pop! Welcome home, Teresa."

Laura smiled at her father and rested her head on his shoulder. The two gazed at the landscape below them. Laura saw a steady stream of tears in her father's eyes, only now realizing how hard this all must be for him. She pressed her face against the window as they touched down and began to taxi. Several people on the plane began to clap, sing, and make the sign of the cross as they celebrated the safe arrival of what had been a long and tough journey.

Laura spied a crowd gathering below, awaiting the arrival of their visitors. She began searching the faces of the young men in the crowd, her eyes settling upon the most handsome of them all.

Laura tapped the window with her finger, "Pop, that's him."

"What? Can you smell him?" he asked, straight-faced but amused.

"Look at him, Pop. He's beautiful."

Vito looked, but he didn't see what Laura saw. Suddenly, he grabbed his daughter's hand, looked her in the eye, and he said, "Laura, you let me know if you don't like him. You hear me. You let me know. I'm serious. You say the word, and we'll take the next plane home. No questions asked."

"The next plane?"

He responded seriously, "Yes, do you hear me?"

"I hear you, Papa. I love you. Thank you." Without taking her eyes off Enzo, she added, "Whatever you say, Pop."

After what seemed an interminably long time, Laura and Vito climbed out onto the rickety stairs on to the tarmac. As soon as she inhaled the cool Italian air, Laura felt an amazing sense of calm. *I am home,* she thought.

Enzo could not even describe the overflow of emotions he felt as he watched yet another plane arrive—this time, one from America. And his heart nearly burst when he realized this plane actually contained Laura. He rushed to Laura's side as soon as father and daughter stepped onto the tarmac. The pair regarded each other, and the world stood still; everything around them melted into a monochromatic backdrop. Laura shifted under the intensity of Enzo's attention.

Vito cleared his throat, and the airport snapped back into focus.

Enzo reluctantly shifted his eyes from Laura to Vito, and extended his hand. "Mr. Baccaro? It's a pleasure to meet you."

Vito regarded him skeptically, a little bewildered by the immediate attraction he could feel between Laura and Enzo. The men shook hands. He tamped down his sudden anger and said cheerfully, "Enzo, my pleasure. This is my daughter, Laura."

Enzo looked at her and said, "Laura, welcome to Italy." He handed her what seemed like a wilted and sad bouquet.

Though dwarfed by Enzo, Laura expanded toward him like a sunflower reaching for the sun. An intense beat passed between them.

Enzo cleared his throat and squared his shoulders. "Mr. Baccaro, do I have permission to kiss your daughter?"

Vito was both taken aback and slightly amused. He looked at his daughter as if looking at her through a telescope. He smiled meekly at her, "What do you think, Laura?"

"I like him, Pop," she replied, her voice almost breathless. Her smile was luminous.

Vito caved. He nodded at Enzo, who beamed at him before turning to Laura.

Enzo bent down and gently kissed her on the cheek.

Laura suddenly burst into startled laughter, dispelling the tension, and Enzo smiled at her. She was completely mesmerized by his eyes. His touch and single kiss sent her into the stratosphere—a place she had never been before.

Later, they walked into the lobby of the small hotel where they would be staying until heading south. Enzo went to the front desk and spoke with the concierge, who quickly disappeared from behind the desk. Laura peered around the lobby, charmed by everything. Her father watched her closely.

There was a flurry of activity from the balcony overlooking the lobby, and Josephina, Enzo's mother, bustled down the stairs. Her frantic excitement garnered all of the attention, and it took a few moments for anyone to notice that she was wearing only a slip.

Enzo laughed heartily. "Ma, you're not dressed!"

Josephina only had eyes for Laura. She kissed her cheeks several times, pulling back frequently to admire her.

Both overwhelmed and charmed by the exuberant affection, Laura looked to Enzo.

Enzo said to Laura, "My mother." He turned to his mother and said laughing, "You'll scare her off!"

Josephina said, "Oh, look at how lovely she is!"

"Mama, this is Vito, Laura's father."

Josephina gave Vito an equally huge, unashamed greeting.

Vito was momentarily embarrassed, but Josephina's sincerity was infectious. "It's a pleasure, Mrs. Fellini."

"Oh, Vito! Call me Josephina, please."

"It's a pleasure to meet you, Mrs. Fellini," Laura managed to get out in her best Italian.

Enzo, Josephina, and Vito shared an appreciative glance at the girl's broken Italian. Josephina simply embraced Laura.

☙❦❧

Later that day, after some rest to adjust to the time change, the foursome decided to take in some local sights. Enzo, Vito, Laura, and Josephina wandered around a beautiful, sunken Roman garden. Lounging and climbing cats were everywhere. The flowers, the abundance of the colors, the scent of the air, and the absolute beauty instantly captivated Laura. She had been deprived of such beauty in

Brooklyn. Her imagination suddenly came to life, and it was jubilant!

Laura and Enzo tried to corner a kitten, after Laura had expressed an interest in petting it. They both laughed hard, exaggerating their gestures to compensate for their lack of full comprehension of the other's language. The chemistry between them was undeniable. If only their eyes could speak. They could not stop looking at each other.

Out of the shadow of their lingering grief over their loss of Teresa, the woman who had brought them all together, all four were giddy with energy. Their emotions all seemingly aligned as they felt Teresa's presence among them, feeling connected to her, at that moment, by her life and death, but mostly by her desire for Enzo and Laura to meet. They shared their stories and their love of Teresa, and even shed a few tears.

Enzo and his mother expressed their gratitude to Laura and Vito for the love and care they had provided Teresa. Enzo spoke of his aunt's loving letters. The pain was evident, but the love far surpassed his sadness at that moment.

Later that day, Enzo and Laura sat on the ledge of a huge fountain. They were momentarily alone. The space between them was magnetic. Enzo moved to push a wisp of hair away from her face, but she pulled away as if the move was expected of her.

She was fearful of his touch. She had never experienced the sensations she was experiencing now. Her senses were heightened in his presence. It was difficult for her to come to terms with her reaction to his closeness and all that he made her feel. She loved his scent, felt tormented by his slightest touch, and relished in his smooth voice and rich accent. She was thrilled to finally hear the voice she had only imagined. The thought of kissing him felt like a distant dream that she still wanted to hold on to. Actually, the thought of kissing him was almost more than she thought she could properly process.

Enzo smiled and put his hands up to show harmlessness.

Laura smiled. She hesitated a moment, and then put her head on his shoulder.

He smiled and didn't move.

"You smell nice," she murmured.

Enzo replied, "I smell?"

Laura sat up, "No! Good. You smell good."

Enzo frowned and sniffed his shirt. "It's not dirty."

"No, Enzo, I like it."

"You like dirty?"

Flustered, Laura protested, "No! Enzo, you smell good. You smell like flowers, like soap. I like it. It's good." She exaggeratedly sniffed him, smiled, and gave him a thumbs up.

He chuckled, and she narrowed her eyes at him.

"Thank you. My mother makes . . . what's the word for *sopane*?"

"Sopane?"

Enzo mimed taking a shower.

Laura giggled. "Oh! Soap!"

Enzo repeated, "Soap! Yes, she sells amazing soap all over Sicily."

Laura pantomimed Enzo's performance, and the pair laughed together, already developing a bond through humor.

❧

Late that evening, after sharing a warm welcome dinner at a local restaurant, the four sluggishly approached the hotel. Josephina and Vito entered the building, while Laura and Enzo hung back. With the disappearance of their parents, Enzo snaked his hand into Laura's. The two shared a moment of intense eye contact. He smiled at her and leaned in. Her eyes went wide, and she stiffened involuntarily.

Enzo noticed her unease and pulled away, laughed and raised his hands to signal his harmlessness once again.

She smiled, embarrassed. An awkward beat passed before she extended her hand to him for a handshake. He took it, amused.

"It's nice to finally meet you, Enzo Fellini."

"The pleasure is all mine, Laura Baccaro."

They shook hands, and both felt the electricity travel up their arms.

Chapter Eight

The next morning, Enzo, Laura, and their respective parents
sat in the passenger car of a train, which hurtled through the
Italian countryside headed for Sicily. Laura and Enzo sat next to each
other, bouncing with energy.

Laura pointed to the trees and asked, "How do you say that?"

"Albero."

"Albero!"

She pointed at the seats in the train, "And this?"

"Sedile."

"Sedile!"

"And that?" she pointed to the windows.

"Finestra."

"Finestra!"

This went on for several hours. Ten hours later, between delays
and scheduled stops, they all felt the wear of travel. Josephina and
Vito slept across the aisle. Enzo was still trying to teach Laura words,
but she had long since stopped listening. She was falling asleep.

"Sognare—Dream. *Perfezione*—Perfection. *Grato*—Grateful." Enzo
repeated these out loud.

"Enzo," Laura mumbled, "I like . . ." before drifting off.

While she slept, Enzo studied her sleepy face in detail, almost
as if he were etching this long-awaited moment in memory. He

scrounged for English words. He found himself saying out loud in English, "Laura, I like as well!"

When Laura finally awoke, Enzo breathed a sigh of relief. He pointed out toward the rapidly passing scenery. "Do you . . . like Italy?" he asked.

"I do. The clouds are bigger here, somehow. They look . . . this may sound silly . . . They look like clouds out of a painting. Clouds here make the clouds from the Renaissance paintings make sense. I like very much."

Enzo still grasped for the English words, "Clouds? You like our Italian clouds? I am flattered. I ordered them to be at their best for the beautiful American girl's arrival!"

Laura laughed. "Yes, I like the clouds, Enzo."

There was an awkward moment.

Enzo said, "Clouds? Very good! Now let's say 'the clouds are beautiful': *le nuvole sono belle. . .* "

Laura repeated, "*Le nuvole sono belle.*"

Enzo told her to repeat, "*Ma non è così bella come me.*"

Laura repeated the phrase, and Enzo smiled at her.

"What did I say?" she asked.

Enzo translated, "That you are more beautiful than the clouds."

Laura's face turned scarlet, and she looked away.

Enzo was consumed with breaking the barriers between them and wanted to learn and communicate with her as clearly as possible, as soon as possible. After all, his whole town was awaiting her arrival. In Enzo's world, her presence there was huge. He knew how he felt about her even before she stepped onto the tarmac. His first sighting only further deepened his feelings.

He also knew she was young and that he should move slowly. He did not want all the attention she would receive in Partanna to overwhelm her, and he felt very protective of her immediately.

Later that night, the foursome stepped off the train in Southern

Italy and lined up to board a ferry to take them to Sicily. Once on the ferry, Laura stood on the deck of the boat, as the wind blew through her hair. Enzo came to stand next to her. She smiled at him, amazed by the beauty of the landscape. It all felt so magical to her. They didn't speak much, but rather just enjoyed each other's closeness.

Once the ferry arrived at its destination, they boarded yet another train that would take them through Alcamo and then to Enzo's hometown. When they arrived in Alcamo early in the morning, the train came to an unexpected stop. The station was unusually crowded with people. Enzo's face lit up with surprise to see that several of his close friends were at this station, apparently there to surprise him, happy that the American had arrived after his three-day wait at the airport in Rome. Word traveled quickly in those small towns.

Laura asked, "What are all these people doing here?"

Vito patted her shoulder in reply. She looked out the window, aghast but excited. Vito did not want to let on to too much, so he minimized his own surprise and alarm at stopping at *this* particular station. His chronic heartburn was about to begin.

The crowd bustled excitedly on the platform. This was a small town, and practically everyone who lived there had come to see the boy who had left many years ago to make it big in the beloved America. However, Vito chose to remain in the car until the train resumed its course.

Enzo said nothing, but thought this all seemed somewhat odd. He emerged from the train first, waving, before dramatically taking Laura's hand and presenting her to the crowd. The crowd erupted in applause, and Laura stood, blinking in surprise. Enzo placed his arm around her shoulders, proud and triumphant.

Laura scowled, resisting the urge to shake him off. She was a bit confused and overwhelmed by his display.

Enzo waved them off, smiling and blushing. He leaned in for a kiss with Laura, but he could feel her tense and changed course at the last minute to kiss her temple instead. A few scattered boos rang out from the crowd, mixed with cheers from some of the women.

The crowd dissolved quickly, once it was clear there was nothing more to see.

Neighborhood gossips trailed within the group, hoping that some new fodder would justify their lingering on. News of the Americans' arrival had traveled quickly. *Unbeknownst to the Americans,* Enzo thought for a second, as he looked out and saw some familiar faces he knew from his town surrounding an older woman dressed in black. They stood off in the distance and he quickly dismissed an unsettling thought, as he could not be certain it was whom he suspected. They would not be here to celebrate this event with him. Of this, he was sure. They should not be in Alcamo today of all days.

His mind was racing with anticipation and thoughts of the formal introduction he was about to make to his town folk and other family members shortly. He knew they would all be there waiting. He was so proud to present Laura Baccaro to all.

Vito, on the other hand, just wanted the train to move. He had been unaware the train would be making a stop in Alcamo. It made him uneasy, it was painful, and he just wanted out as soon as possible. No good could come from his being here. Thirty minutes later, Enzo's few friends joined the group in the passenger car, and the train finally left the station. Vito was able to breathe freely again.

Once the train pulled into the Partanna station, the scene reenacted itself. An even larger crowd had gathered, all eager to welcome the visitors. The clamor of accordion music, singing, dancing, and cheers of delight nearly bowled the Americans over. Flowers, food, and ecstatic hugs and kisses abounded. Laura felt like a movie star.

Vito gave his daughter a look and said, "Eh, Laura, don't let it go to your head. All these people could be crazy."

They both laughed.

"You know, you just never know," she replied.

Laura felt frazzled, but she couldn't help but soak up the beautiful countryside as all of this was going on. She was flattered, amused, and taken back by all of this attention. Enzo was so protective and gentle with her. Everyone was so very kind. Laura felt blessed.

"Thank you, Papa," she said, clasping Vito's hand.

It took a while to escape the crowd, but once they did, Laura became misty eyed at the sight of Enzo's charming house. She was actually standing in the spot she had only imagined and dreamed of for so long.

The house was immaculate, nestled just so on an amazing countryside of hills and valleys with clear views from every angle. The view was breathtaking, just the way she had envisioned it. The garden was spectacular, with an array of gorgeous sunflowers standing at attention in welcome. The use of decorative stone added a warm texture to a home that was clearly worn but felt immediately friendly and so welcoming. To her, it felt so intimate to finally be in his space and in his family's home.

Enzo waved at the followers, bid them farewell, and thanked them for such support. A few shook Laura's hand or kissed her cheek, but most congratulated Enzo in some way.

As the friends and followers left, Vito, Laura, Enzo and Josephina along with a few of Enzo's extended family entered the endearing house.

Giovanni appeared in the front room to greet the visitors. Josephina went to him and kissed him swiftly on both cheeks, speaking to him rapidly in Italian before she disappeared into the kitchen. Giovanni was an impressive, commanding man. He shook Vito's hand and embraced him for what seemed an eternity. He was indebted to him for the care he had given his sister.

He turned his attention to Laura, as she extended her hand to him to shake it, but he took her hand and spun her around to size her up. Laura snatched her hand back, mortified, and Giovanni laughed. He looked her up and down again before nodding. He clapped Enzo on the back proudly.

Then he embraced Laura tightly and squealed. This would be the first time Laura would hear Giovanni squeal with delight. He had a precise, singsong way of emitting a sound that was full of glee, an irrefutable signature of approval and happiness. Laura would come to know this sound well.

Giovanni was a loving and happy man, deep down inside. He stopped at nothing to please others and give all he could. His heart was full of love, but his sister's situation, from leaving Italy to passing away in America, had all but broken his heart.

Along with Giovanni, Laura was introduced to Enzo's younger brother, Pedro, whom Enzo had affectionately written about on many occasions, and Francesca, his married sister. The excitement and warm welcome were precious. Laura was sure that this would be one of those moments in life she would remember forever. She felt so much love that it was almost magical. The day could not have gone any better for her, she realized, but there was so much to absorb and process.

Enzo smiled at Laura apologetically. He was concerned that it all could be too much for her. He had been very in tune with everything that had transpired that day, and he noticed that she looked on the verge of tears.

Enzo tried to take her arm to lead her further into the house, but she pulled her arm away and marched in by herself. She felt a myriad of overwhelming emotions, but under it all, she felt immense gratitude for Teresa's foresight. She just did not understand the intensity of all the new, varied emotions she was starting to feel.

The next day, Laura stood by the sun-flooded window in the small bedroom given to her for her stay. It was so beautiful she could hardly breathe. She turned and noticed a colorful package on the dresser with her name on it. She untied a piece of twine that held together a piece of crimson paper, and revealed a small bar of cream-colored soap. She smiled as she inhaled the fragrance. It smelled like Teresa.

Chapter Nine

*L*aura stood at the terrace door and watched Enzo sitting at the small table with appreciation and awe. He stared at the mountains and hummed to himself. She smiled and stepped into the sunlight. Feeling her presence, Enzo looked up and stopped humming. She glowed, and Enzo could barely look at her.

She stood awkwardly for a moment before speaking. "What were you humming?"

Confused, Enzo said, "*Buongiorno, bella.* Humming?"

Laura hummed the bit of the tune she heard. He smiled and started to sing Frank Sinatra's "All or Nothing at All." He sang with relish and without self-consciousness.

Laura smiled, loving his voice, and went to Enzo, pulled him to his feet, and he held his arms out for a dance. She stiffened, but was ready to comply.

Giovanni stomped out onto the patio. "No. No dancing, Enzo. You know that. Respect your wonderful aunt's soul."

Enzo clenched his jaw and dropped his hands. Laura watched Giovanni stomp back into the house. She looked at Enzo confused.

He sighed. "My father . . . he is very old fashioned. No celebration for six months after a death. No singing. No dancing. If it were solely up to him, he would mourn her forever. Thank God my grandfather sees it much differently."

"Oh, Teresa. Sweet Teresa. I understand," Laura replied. But to herself, she was sorry Giovanni hadn't come out a few minutes later. She had almost been in Enzo's arms.

Enzo smiled sadly. A moment later, Enzo's grandfather joined them on the patio, with Vito close behind.

Laura knew immediately that she would love this man named Peter. He was a man who knew the earth well. He had a weathered look from spending most of his days outdoors. He was rugged and old, and Laura was sure that at one time he must have been very handsome. She would soon learn that Peter never wore a watch because he could read the sun. He could also read the moon and the stars. He was interesting, smart, and full of wisdom. He looked at Laura and gave her a warm hug.

"Your goodness shines," he said to her. "I love you already. I am with you and welcome you and your family to our home. I heard my son, Giovanni, tell Enzo not to dance. Well, I have news for you. Teresa is up there dancing. I see her. She said to dance and sing. She is so happy you are here. She said you loved her and cared for her when she was alive and without family. You provided her with the things we could not give. How do we repay you for that?"

With that, he went to Vito and gave him a huge kiss on the cheek and said, "That was from Teresa. From me, I will forever be in your debt. You will never know what it has all meant to us."

He hurried away to retrieve his private stash of homemade wine, and when he returned, they all toasted their arrival and Teresa.

"To Teresa!" Peter said. *"Si prega di guarde su di noi in questo giorno."* (Please watch over us on this day.)

He continued to speak to Enzo and Laura. "When you hear the music in your heart, you dance. In case you cannot see, Teresa is dancing right beside you."

Laura marveled at this man. She thought he was fantastic. It was as though he knew all Teresa had written to her in that final letter. Still, as happy as those words made her, she would not betray Giovanni's wishes.

Moments later, other family members and friends intermittently started arriving to meet Laura. One of the visitors was Teresa's only son. His name was Nero. He was very unlike Teresa or his sisters. Laura quickly noticed that he was stern and serious, and that felt very unwelcoming to Laura. He immediately felt it important to point out that this was a time of mourning for his family. No music, drinking, or dancing should be included in this celebration.

Laura was taken aback, but delighted to see that Peter was not in agreement and made faces and amusing gestures behind the younger Nero's back. Peter elevated everyone's spirits and felt they should honor Teresa's life, not mourn her loss. He was uplifting, and Laura felt delighted to be in his presence.

The next day, Enzo drove Laura and Vito to the marketplace. Laura was seated in the passenger seat and a seemingly oblivious Vito sat between them. They eased to a stop at the Trapani Outdoor Market and parked.

Vito meandered through the market, charmed by all the familiar aromas. Enzo wandered a bit, as Laura followed her father. She listened as he openly reminisced about the amazing fresh fruits and vegetables. Some he had not seen in years as they were only available in Italy. He still longed for these items in America.

Vito relished the opportunity to teach Laura about some of the traditional foods. He was thoroughly enjoying this time with his daughter, and part of him wished he had her all to himself to share this experience with. He found himself being a little dismissive of Enzo and struggled to ignore how much Laura seemed drawn to the young man. Enzo was a good boy, from a working-class family. Vito did not want Laura to be disappointed. She was so young. If he were being honest, he didn't want her to set her sights on anyone. She had many more years before he thought she would be ready for marriage. And when the time for marriage did come, it would be to a man with potential, one that could offer her a good life. Of that, he would make sure. *This Enzo is clouding her head,* he thought, just as Enzo approached the father and daughter. Vito was not ready to lose her.

"Vito, I was wondering," Enzo said, hesitating just a bit, "with your permission, if I could show Laura something while you shop."

Vito tore his appreciative gaze away from the prickly pears on the table, and said, "Of course, let's go."

"Well, I was hoping . . ." Enzo paused and motioned in Laura's direction.

Vito clenched his jaw and frowned. It was clear to him they wanted to be alone, and although he wanted to say no, he reluctantly let them go.

"Pazzi ragazzini," he muttered, as the pair hurried away.

Vito moved further on in the market. His thoughts brought him to his childhood and all the wonderful days he had spent in the Alcamo markets. He felt bittersweet nostalgia. His mind then turned toward the reason he had stayed away these past thirty years. Suddenly, he heard the voice. *That* voice. And his blood curdled. Had she seen him? Was the stress of this trip igniting an overactive imagination? He ducked behind one of the carts.

"Hey, Vito, is that you?" called an unfamiliar voice.

Vito looked around and saw an aged man. Although recognizable as a distant cousin, he pretended he hadn't heard the call and headed in the opposite direction. He was not ready to face these upsetting emotions. Instead, he let them fester within. He held nothing against this cousin, but thought, *What the hell. I have lived without him for this long.* Uncertain about his feelings, he had not yet resolved if the urge to kill Maria had passed. He figured he'd play it safe and avoid any confrontation.

❧❦❧

Enzo and Laura climbed up the side of an overgrown hill. A small dirt path had been trampled into the brush. They crested the hill, and Laura caught her breath at the view. They stood above a span-ning valley that turned gold in the early evening sunlight and the ocean glittered in the background.

Laura slowly noticed her surroundings. She stood in a lush, per-fectly maintained garden, a ruggedly beautiful Eden with colorful clusters of wildflowers and fruit-heavy olive trees. She looked around herself in amazement before her eyes found a nervous-looking Enzo.

"This is yours? Yours?" she asked.

Enzo nodded, and Laura laughed happily, wiping tears from her eyes. "It's beautiful, Enzo," she said. *"E bello,"* she repeated. She was amazed by how emotional she had been feeling.

She surveyed the view, shaking her head in wondrous amaze-ment. She walked up to a gnarled old olive tree. She looked at Enzo mischievously and found foot holes in the tangle of branches, then slipped up and into a tree.

She called over her shoulder, *"His Girl Friday!"*

This movie title was a reference to the game they'd played during their letter writing. Enzo and Laura had been seriously invested in the dialogue of the movies Laura watched and those that Enzo pro-jected. They'd made a game of sharing their favorite lines. They never imagined this commonality would help them forge a deeper understanding of one another.

Enzo's eyes sparkled with understanding, and he tried to find her in the blossoming branches. He replied, "I'd know you any time, any place, anywhere!"

Laura called out, *"Casablanca!"*

Enzo stuck his feet in the trunk and hoisted himself into the tree saying, "Here's looking at you, kid!"

Laura said, *"Wizard of Oz!"*

Enzo climbed until he faced her and said, "There's no place like home! *Non c'e'nessun posto come a casa."*

Enzo looked up into the tree and then back at Laura, mischief gleamed in his eyes. He climbed higher, grasping frighteningly unstable branches, and Laura smiled when she saw what he was going for—a sprig of white flowers growing at the top of the tree.

He reached the flowers and delicately plucked a full white blossom before careening back to Laura. He gave her the flower with a flourish, and she laughed, charmed, and asked, "What's the word? Name?"

He said, *"Fiori d'oliva."*

Laura smiled and repeated, *"Fiori d'oliva."* She relished the simplicity of the moment.

His attention became suddenly very intense. He placed the flower behind her ear, leaving his hand on her neck. Chills ran up and down her spine.

"Laura."

Not knowing how to withstand his intense gaze, she leaned over and picked a sprig of small bright green leaves. She tucked the sprig into a buttonhole in his shirt. Her hand lingered on his chest. A kiss was imminent.

The moment was interrupted by a loud *humpf.* Vito had made it to the top of the hill, huffing and puffing and looking overall frustrated. He bellowed, "Laura! What the hell are you doing up there? You could hurt yourself."

Enzo hopped out of the tree, and Laura followed, less gracefully than he but equally full of energy. Enzo caught her, and they stood for a moment, holding on to each other.

Vito cleared his throat loudly, breaking Enzo and Laura apart. *"Amore folle—*this crazy love—is going to kill me!"

Laura turned a deep scarlet, but asked her father, "Isn't it beautiful, Pop?" She wondered if could read her mind and tell what she was wishing for.

Vito responded, "It looks like wasted space to me." He looked straight at Enzo and said, *"Lo sono di vecchio per questo,* Enzo. I am too old for this."

Laura sighed and tried to laugh, but her happy mood deflated under Vito's grumpiness. She was uncertain about exactly when he'd gone from relaxed to this agitated mood of his or even why.

Vito surveyed the landscape, annoyed. Enzo tried to mask his disappointment by pretending to prune a bush. Laura felt frustrated by her father's timing and sudden dourness, and began to feel that they would never have time enough alone to fully get to know each other.

❦

Once back in the truck, Vito sat, again, between Enzo and Laura. All three looked annoyed and tired.

They pulled up in front of Enzo's little theater. Enzo cut the engine and looked like he was about to say something when Vito scoffed, not seeing Enzo's hopeful, proud expression, and said, "See, Laura. Look at how sad that is. It's poverty like that that drove your mama and me to leave. It is not as prosperous here as it is in America. The *Stati Uniti* offers so many opportunities."

Laura knew her parents had both been very young when they left Italy, but Enzo did not. She felt her father had said this more to impress upon her the opportunities she had in the United States than to put Enzo on the defensive. Still, Enzo's face fell, and he started the truck again.

Vito asked, "What were you going to show us?"

Enzo responded, "Nothing," and began to drive away.

Laura's eye caught the marquee. "Oh! Enzo! Is this where you. . . . You work here?" She sounded surprised and a bit taken aback.

Enzo shrugged and shook his head, disheartened. He loved his theater. He felt ashamed that these Americans could not appreciate its worth.

❦

That night, feeling exhausted, everyone at the Fellini house went bed early. They would start over the next day, feeling refreshed.

When Enzo woke up in the morning, he felt renewed and had a plan to impress his new American friends. They would all go on an all-day excursion—Vito, Laura, his parents, and him. He would take the lead.

They spent the day visiting museums, churches, outdoor markets, and seaside vineyards. They drank wine. They ate olives. They had fresh baked bread, gelato, pizza, and cannolis. Enzo gave Laura and Vito the true tourist experience. They laughed, shared stories, bonded, and by the end of the day, Enzo felt it had been a true success. Things were going in the right direction. Vito seemed much more peaceful and receptive to being in his homeland.

Chapter Ten

The next day, Enzo, Laura, and Vito made stops at a few more local tourist attractions, but the itinerary was not as intense as it had been the day before. Spirits were high, and connections, in Enzo's mind, were easily being made. Over all, the day passed seamlessly. Before returning to the house for dinner, they stopped to see Peter in the fields where he tended his animals. Vito and Laura, and Enzo as well, were again amused and entertained and quite impressed by Peter's abilities, intelligence, and progressive insights of life. He was quite simply an amazing man.

Finally back from their excursion, the tired trio filed into the front room. Enzo's friend, Sophia, appeared from the kitchen. She was tall, beautiful, and seemingly self-confident. Laura never expected Enzo to have such a beautiful friend, and she immediately felt a pang of jealousy. Her self-confidence evaporated. She stood a little straighter.

When Enzo saw Sophia, his mood immediately brightened. "Who invited you?" he asked playfully, embracing her.

Sophia laughed and pushed on him playfully. She stood on her tiptoes to slip her arm over his shoulders and lean on him.

Laura pursed her lips and played with her hair.

"Your mother invited me for dinner to meet your new friends from America, of course," she replied.

Enzo turned to Laura to make an introduction, with Sophia still hanging from him. "Laura, this is Sophia, my dear friend.

Sophia responded with lightning-quick Italian, "Very nice to meet you, Laura. How do you like Partanna?"

Laura looked at her blankly. She clenched her jaw before she shrugged her shoulders and looked at Enzo for help translating.

He smiled and turned to Sophia. "She doesn't follow Italian very well. We are both still practicing. You just need to speak a little slower. Or speak in English."

Sophia raised her eyebrow at Enzo and stifled a smirk. Laura caught the facial expression and clenched her jaw. Enzo didn't notice the exchange as he rubbed Laura on the shoulder. He pointed to the kitchen.

"My mother," he said, "she has asked for you in kitchen. She wants to show you how she prepares her specialty, *Pollo al Marsala.*"

Laura raised an eyebrow at Enzo. She opened her mouth to say something, but changed her mind. Her face red with embarrassment, she marched out of the room. She felt agitated, but she could not fully determine why. She had never felt like this before. Enzo watched her go, a little confused.

Sophia said quietly to Enzo, "Can't speak Italian? This is your American romance?"

"Be nice," he said. "Have some compassion."

Sophia responded, "No, no, I understand. I wouldn't want to talk to her either." She flashed him a big, fake smile and meandered toward the kitchen as well.

Confused and irritated by Sophia's mood, Enzo followed her into the kitchen.

❧

The six people enjoyed an intimate dinner around the cozy wooden table. Josephina bustled around, serving course after course and cleaning as she went. When speaking directly to Laura, they would speak slowly and use as much English as they knew, but otherwise, the Italian conversation flowed naturally, and she simply tried to follow along.

"So, Sophia, how do you know Enzo?" Vito asked in Italian, apparently charmed by the guest and what she might represent in Enzo's life.

Sophia replied, "Enzo and I have been friends since we were babies."

Enzo added, "We used to race to school."

"I always won," Sophia quipped.

Enzo laughed. "You always won, but then you were too out of breath to do anything else."

Sophia replied, "Yes, but I beat you."

Vito laughed at the exchange and said, "It's nice to see you have such a good friend here."

Enzo said, "She's been with this family through some big moments."

Laura picked at her food, frustrated by the quickness of this exchange. She followed along as best as she could, but she could only be sure of the body language and hadn't missed how many times Sophia had touched Enzo's arm or glanced at him in a certain way. Her mood was declining rapidly.

She noticed suddenly that she was in physical pain—an unfamiliar pain in her lower abdomen and lower back. It had been slight the past few days, but it was starting to grow in intensity now. Suddenly, she felt incredibly insecure and miserable. *Why tonight, of all nights, did I have to meet this amazingly beautiful girl?* she thought with a sinking heart. She could not understand what was happening to her body or her emotions. She had never felt this erratic.

In the sea of tanned skin, Laura stood out as exceptionally pale. She looked at her forearm a bit self-consciously and eyed Sophia's tanned complexion. She played with her hair, trying to pull her waves straight like Sophia's.

Laura became gradually more upset as the conversation continued. If she hadn't been so upset, she might have had half a chance at concentrating clearly. It was all these distracting thoughts that threw her off course. Laura and Enzo had seemed to have created a momentum. The communication was not yet perfect, but it was working. Throwing a new person into the mix disoriented her, especially when the new person looked like Sophia.

Enzo continued, "And she was here for another big day in my life: when I met Laura, my beautiful American girl!" Enzo leaned toward Laura and looked like he might kiss her.

Laura impulsively sprang out of her chair. She knew he had said all the appropriate things, but suddenly, she was unable to contain herself any longer.

"Enzo! Stop it!" she said.

The table hushed. She glared at Enzo, Sophia, and then at her father.

"Why am I here? Why am I even *here*?!" she exclaimed and marched out the door. There was a stunned silence before Enzo jumped up and ran after her.

Laura stormed angrily away from the house. It was a warm evening, with a low milky moon over the hills. Enzo ran out the door and watched her for a moment before taking off at a jog to catch up with her. She didn't acknowledge him. He kept pace with her, somewhat amused by her frustration.

"Where did you learn to walk so fast?" he asked.

"Go away," she ordered.

"I don't think I've ever made someone this mad. I don't even know what I've done!"

Laura ignored him, and they walked in silence.

Enzo began to grow uneasy. "Where are you going?"

"Stop following me," she responded.

Enzo continued as if he didn't hear her. "When I was a kid, I used to run around these streets, jumping onto passing trucks . . ."

Laura suddenly stopped walking. She turned to him with fire in her eyes and cut him off angrily, "Stop it! Stop talking!" She breathed hard, on the verge of tears.

Enzo's cheerfulness fully dissolved. "Laura . . ." He walked over to her and tried to embrace her.

"STOP!" she said angrily and pushed him away.

Caught off guard, he stumbled several steps backward. He raised his hands in defeat. He waited a beat and asked, "What happened?"

Laura asked, "You love me, *tu mi ami?*"

Enzo responded, "Yes."

She scoffed and turned to walk away.

Enzo desperately said, "Yes. Yes, Laura! Yes!"

"Per sempre?" Laura asked with sarcasm dripping from her voice.

Enzo brightened and trotted after her. *"Per sempre!"*

Laura stopped and turned to face him. "Why?" she asked.

Confused he repeated, "Why?"

Laura responded, "Why."

Enzo started to speak, "What kind of question . . ."

"In English!" Laura demanded.

Frustrated and angry, Enzo responded, "I can't! You know I can't, not now under this situation! It will not be perfect. *Non sto perfetto.*"

They regarded each other for another tense, frustrated beat. She turned and walked away. He looked at her, taken aback, before following her.

Enzo tried, "Do you really not feel this? Am I crazy? Laura, didn't you fly across the world for me? Didn't we write letters for a year and a half? Laura, *per sempre* means FOREVER!"

He caught up to her and whirled her around.

She looked at him, frustrated to the point of tears, and said, "Not good enough, Enzo! Not in English enough! How am I supposed to like you when I can't even talk to you? She is right, *la tua ragazzaa italiana*—your Italian girlfriend."

She turned and marched away from him, muttering furiously under her breath.

Enzo called after her, "Laura, wait! Stop! That is not so . . . . She is a sister to me. *Abbiamo fatto sapere che avrebbe sconovolto cosi. Avremmo mai lei Inited.* I didn't know she would have upset you so. I would not have let my mother invite her."

Enzo was speaking in whatever language he could get out faster. He caught up to her, but she didn't stop. He stood in front of her and said, "Too dark. You can't. No, no Laura!"

"Watch me," she snapped. She sidestepped him and started walking. Enzo trotted behind her. Finally, over her shoulder, she said, "I'm not going back with you, Enzo."

"It's dangerous. I'm serious."

"*I'm* serious. Don't follow me."

She picked up her pace. He walked behind her for a few steps and then stopped. Her shoulders tensed, but she didn't turn around.

Enzo deliberated with himself for a second. He turned as if to go back to his house. Laura didn't stop. Enzo shook his head. He couldn't let her just walk off into the night. He turned around and jogged to her. He stood in her way, holding his hands up for her to stop. She tried to walk around him, but he stayed a foot in front of her. He tried to put his hands on her shoulders, but she shook him off. They awkwardly danced around each other, growing more frustrated and angry.

Enzo put his hands up, "Laura, please."

She looked at him with disdain, and her look wilted him. He put his hands down. She ran past him, and he reached out to grab her around the waist. She whipped around and slapped him across the face. They looked at each other, stunned.

After a moment, Enzo took off his sweater and held it out to her.

"It's cold. Cold, here please take this," Enzo said.

"Cold," Laura repeated. She took it warily. She stared at it balled up in her fist before she turned away from Enzo and headed out into the night.

He watched her for a moment before he broke into a wild sprint in the direction of his house.

Laura looked over her shoulder and watched him go.

He rounded a bend, and she breathed a sigh of relief. Her sigh turned into a choked sobs, and she held back tears, which confused and annoyed her, and she continued on in to the night. She had no plan and nowhere to go, and she really didn't care at this point.

Chapter Eleven

Enzo had turned away, hoping to scare her out of her irrational behavior and fully expecting her to follow him. When he saw that she hadn't, Enzo raced more quickly toward the house to get the truck, planning to pull up beside her and then take her for a ride to clear the air. But as he ran, his mind played tricks with him. He saw himself in the silky darkness, running like a chased animal. Snatches of his imagination: Laura falling down a hill, a shadowy man coming up behind her, a truck rounding a bend with Laura stuck in the head-lights. His mind was reeling and his thoughts were spinning.

The headlights from Enzo's imagination became real, as they swept the road and landed their beam on Laura. A stranger's truck stopped. Antonio—a neighbor of Vito's brother, Dominick, whom Laura had yet to meet—poked his head out of the window.

"What are you doing out here? You know it's not safe out here for a young girl!" he said.

Laura looked at him and waved him away.

Antonio turned the truck around and drove slowly beside her.

"American?" Antonio asked.

Laura nodded.

"From New York? Is your name Laura by any chance?"

Laura nodded again, growing a little uneasy. He was getting uncomfortably close, and she was now finally starting to question leaving the safety of the Fellini home.

"I am Antonio! Your uncle Dominick, he is my neighbor!" he said excitedly.

Laura came to a stop. "You know my uncle? Is that how you knew I was the American girl?"

"Mr. Dominick, yes, come, I take you to him! He is not far."

"Oh, no, I shouldn't," Laura replied uneasily.

As she spoke, a new thought entered her mind. *It* would *be interesting to meet my uncle. Perhaps I can repair whatever is between him and my Pop and bring him back to the house with me this evening. That would show Enzo I can take care of myself! And my father could see his brother.*

As she contemplated this, Antonio said, "If you don't feel comfortable, I will take you wherever you want to go. But you definitely should not be out here alone."

Laura chewed her lip, debating. She was trusting and thought Antonio's answer was sufficient enough to get in to a truck with him. She glanced at the balled sweater in her fist and rolled her eyes. She nodded to Antonio and said to herself, *Why not?*

He smiled and enthusiastically pulled open the passenger door for her. She slid in and slammed the door shut. As soon as she did, all she could think was that this was a mistake. *I want my pop,* she thought as a surge of fear went through her veins. "Please take me back, I've changed my mind."

Antonio laughed a bit, as friendly as he could muster. "Oh, you are fine!" he said, ignoring her request. He couldn't believe his luck. He had been at the Alcamo train station the day Laura and her father had arrived. He had seen Enzo scanning the group of them standing with Maria, but Enzo had seemed too excited to care to investigate any further. Antonio had seen Laura that day and had studied her face very well. He had been scoping out the house this evening per Maria's bidding and plotting their next move, never expecting this perfect opportunity to present itself so soon.

The plan is moving way ahead of schedule now, he thought. Maybe he would be able to collect his fee now, rather than later. Maybe Maria would even throw in a bonus for this unexpected gift of fate. He smiled as he drove off.

꩜

Moments later, Enzo tumbled in and stumbled to Giovanni.

Vito asked, "Where's Laura?"

Enzo turned to Giovanni and said, "The truck! I need the truck!"

He gave a quick explanation of what had just occurred, and Giovanni grabbed the keys and tossed them to Vito.

Vito marched determinedly out the door and hurried to climb into the truck. Enzo went to get into the cab with him. Vito snarled angrily.

Pained, Enzo said, "Please, I know where she is."

Vito started the truck as Enzo clambered in. They took off with a squeal of tires.

It was tense between the two men, but their mutual worry over Laura and the speed of the truck were enough to keep them from talking. Enzo was nervous almost to the point of tears. He was craned forward in his seat as if willing the truck forward.

Vito said in a low menacing whisper, "You can't have her if she doesn't want you."

Enzo winced, but said, "She should be around here."

Vito slowed the truck. The headlights combed the ground. Enzo leaned out the window so far he looked as if he might fall out.

꩜

When Antonio turned the truck in the opposite direction of where she had just come from, Laura gently pleaded and asked, "Where are you going? Please take me back to my poppa."

Again, he simply laughed and told her not to worry and that he had it all under control. They drove and drove on very dark and mountainous roads. She knew she was incapable of ever finding her way back. Finally, he turned the truck into the driveway of Dominick's house. Darkness swallowed up the countryside, surrounding Laura on all sides. She had never experienced darkness this dark before.

Antonio must have seen Laura looking around in awe. He had tried—unsuccessfully—to make small talk with her on the ride. Laura thought that he seemed harmless but not too bright. *He promised to return me to Partanna if my uncle Dominick is not at home,* she thought hopefully. *I hope no one is home.*

He abruptly stopped the truck and ran to her door to escort her out of the truck. He stayed very close to her side—unusually close. They went to the front door and knocked. She noticed the beads of sweat forming over his bushy eyebrows. He also seemed to be poking his chest out, in a distorted sort of way. Prancing like a peacock. Laura had not noticed this behavior in the truck.

Enzo and Vito parked the truck and resumed their search for Laura on foot, enlisting a couple of strangers they encountered along the way. The countryside was slowly becoming dotted with candlelight and flashlights. Vito's voice was hoarse and wild as he shouted, "Laura! Laura! Laura, are you trying to kill me?"

Vito felt incredibly conflicted. He berated himself for ever agreeing to Teresa's request. His thoughts were a cycle of pure repetition: *I will have to kill Enzo if anything happens to my daughter, Caterina is going to kill me, this is simply not believable, this is why I should have stayed away, how stupid that boy is to have left her for even a moment.* Vito repeated his last thought, out loud this time.

Enzo responded, "I really believed she would be scared and would follow me. She was so upset, there was no stopping her. I think meeting Sophia and my friendship with her confused her."

Both men remained somber as they continued the search.

The door swung open, and dim light poured out of the house. Maria, Laura's aunt by marriage, stood in the doorway. She was a scowling, unattractive woman who had clear evidence of a mustache, upon which, it seemed, an attempt had been made to provide some sort of camouflage. In Laura's mind, it failed. It was crusty even in this evening's dim light.

Maria was surprised to see Antonio at this hour, but still she greeted him with a kiss on each cheek. That was when Laura noticed the coarse waviness of her salt-and-pepper hair, and the mole that existed on the lower portion of her chin from which grew a very long, single strand of black coarse hair.

Laura determined quickly that she did not like the vibe of this lady. She was heavy, dressed in dark clothing, and rather depressing to look at. That one, spiny hair really irritated Laura. She became fixated on it.

Since her youth, Laura had a keen eye and learned to appreciate the finer things in life. She was never able to relate to people who presented themselves in this way. Even if the finer luxuries were not afforded to her personally, she had a keen sense of what was and was not in vogue. Because her mama and sister sewed, she and Ana were always dressed to the nines. Laura had learned so much from her sister and the standards she lived by. She thought for a moment that, at some point, she could make a few suggestions and perhaps buy her a much-needed pair of scissors, razor, or tweezers.

"I picked up a stray," Antonio said. "Look, I found Laura from America,"

Maria's eyes went wild, and she stared at Laura. "Laura? Really, this is her? The precious American I keep hearing about?"

Maria stepped partially into the night. She made it clear she was not inviting Laura inside by her protective body language. She also perked up her stance once she was sure no one else was in earshot. Laura nodded shyly in reply. In a fluid motion, Maria stepped further outside and closed the front door tightly behind her, then she turned and crushed Laura in an enormous hug.

"Thank you so much for bringing her," she said to Antonio. "When we are done here, would you mind taking her to the Russo's, pronto? I did not anticipate this so quickly, but they are prepared to receive her, I am sure."

Laura noticed a slow whine in Maria's voice when she spoke. It almost sounded like she was in pain or was about to cry. Her scent was a mix of terrible perfume with a hint of body odor. Her aunt offended all of her senses almost immediately.

"Of course, no problem," Antonio replied, a hint of surprise in his voice.

Maria turned to Laura and said, almost in a whisper, "Laura, I am so happy to finally meet you. I heard so much about you. All I hear about is *you.*"

Laura tried to respond with, "Yes, we arrived a few days ago. It feels like weeks already."

Maria cut her off. "Is it true that you come to Italy to marry someone who is no good?" she said, her voice becoming cold as ice. "Someone who is not from your own family's town? No, no, Laura. You let me help you. I have a worthy and deserving boy set aside for you. Your father is crazy to let you think alone!"

Laura, stunned, could not think of a way to respond.

"By the way," Maria continued slyly, "how do you get along with Ana? You do know that she is only your half-sister, no?" She repeated this bombshell once more to make sure Laura fully understood. Then she muttered something that sounded like, "She should have been mine," but Laura was sure she had misheard.

When Laura shook her head, indicating that she had indeed not known this information, Maria continued, "Your parents, they kept a *big* secret from you. What does that say for them? Your father, he was married before. Ana only has half your blood. Her mother was crazy. Is she crazy, too? Your sister, she was like my own. I would have saved her from a terrible fate. Your father, he ruined my life, he ruined the life she could have had. But I will fix everything now. I will right this terrible wrong. Poor Dominick still mourns his little girl. He must never, never know the truth."

Laura fully heard her aunt's words but couldn't grasp their full import. Then, Laura decided to ask about Uncle Dominick to get off this crazy train and emphatically added that she had to get back to Enzo's house, but Maria kept on speaking over her, louder and louder in her horrid voice.

"Don't worry about Dominick. He is asleep and there is no need to disturb him. I'm sending you to stay the night at my cousin's house." Laura detected that this was another boldfaced lie. "You can't stay here. Make sure you give Alfonso this, and he'll know what to do with you."

Maria pulled a small piece of paper from her pocket and gave it to Antonio. "These are the notes we all discussed a few days ago. Now go to my cousin's, sweetie. We talk more in the morning. I will fix everything. Your father is blind, and I cannot allow you to come to our town and destroy the family's reputation."

She hugged Laura again before she slipped into the house. "I won't let you ruin your future," she said, just before the door closed. The scent of her breath blew into Laura's face. Laura wanted to vomit.

"Take me back, now," she ordered Antonio. "You said you would bring me to Uncle Dominick or wherever I wanted to go! This lady is crazy. She could not possibly be married to my uncle."

"You heard her," said Antonio. "I cannot do that. Get in the truck, Laura. I will take you to Alfonso. Know that you will be safe there."

"Who on earth is Alfonso?" Laura shrieked. "I am going back to my papa! You promised! Take me back *now!*"

Antonio ignored her request and shoved her into the truck. He was much larger, and she thought it best not to try to fight him. He frightened her in some way, but somehow she didn't think he wanted to physically hurt her. He said she would be safe with Alfonso, and if that meant getting safely away from Antonio—and that insane woman—then so be it. He drove her as he was instructed to do, straight to the Russo's home.

Once there, he told her to get out of the truck, and, feeling as if she had little choice, she did as he said. He knocked on the front door. The house was dark, but sizable, perched on the top of a hill not far from Maria's home.

An unusually short, muscular man of about twenty-five years opened the door and blinked away sleep. He looked quizzically at the visitors. Laura noticed that his hair seemed to add about three inches of height to his head. It looked as though it grew vertically and then curled.

"Sorry to bother you, Alfonso," Antonio began, "but please take Laura off my hands. I have plans and I have to go. Good luck. Oh, yeah, this is Laura from America. You know what you have to do. Here are Maria's instructions."

With that, Antonio hurried back to the truck, leaving Laura behind. Now that he had scored points with Maria and would be paid for his efforts, he didn't seem too interested anymore.

Again, not knowing what other choice she had, Laura asked about Maria's note to Alfonso. He read it quickly before he looked back at Laura, his eyes wide and surprised as if he expected her to run away. "What does that note say, what is this about?"

"Laura?" he asked. "Oh my goodness, Laura. Laura, come in. Come in, please . . ."

She nodded, wary of his reaction. Alfonso opened the door wide for her, and with a backward glance at Antonio's retreating truck, she stepped into the dark house.

Laura stood in the living room, suddenly exhausted. The house was quiet and dark. There was evidence that a large family that lived here: photographs, jackets and shoes, a long dining room table. She turned to Alfonso. He stood behind her, watched her explore the room. He smiled bashfully at her. Every move she made, he countered, so that he was always between her and the door. She narrowed her eyes at him. They stood in the dark room awkwardly, each distrustful of the other.

Alfonso moved first, walked past her to cross the living room. He stopped at the doorway, looked over his shoulder, and waved her toward him. She didn't move. He smiled. He reached for a heavy iron candlestick that stood on the mantle, removed the candle, and handed the candlestick to her. She looked at him quizzically.

"If I make a wrong move . . ." He pointed to the candlestick and then to the back of his head.

Laura tested the weight of the candlestick and then smiled. "Deal," she replied.

He smiled at her and disappeared into the hallway.

Laura took a deep breath and followed him further into the house. Alfonso showed her to a room. It was clean and comfortable, but once she stepped inside, he locked her in.

She realized instantly that she had walked right into this situation by fleeing from Enzo and ignoring his warnings. She was filled with regret, fear, embarrassment, and suddenly, severe cramping.

⁊⁊

Several hours later, Vito and Enzo were exhausted, having scrambled all over the countryside. Their helpers had dwindled and gone home to bed. Vito was crazed with worry. The sun started to rise.

A motorcycle came flying around the corner. Enzo dove in front of the driver, who skidded to a stop in a wave of dust. The driver jumped off his bike and started shouting at Enzo. Enzo, taut with anxiety, snapped and yelled back.

Enzo had recognized the driver as one of the men from days earlier at the Alcamo train stop. "Just tell me if you've seen a girl wandering around these parts!" he shouted.

The guy laughed at him and said, "Is this what you do for fun, Enzo? Look for innocent girls in the night? Ha!" he said, and then he spat in Enzo's face.

Enzo lunged at him, knocking him to the ground, and Vito quickly intervened. Blood dripped from a gash above the thug's eyebrow. Vito scrambled between the two men, shoving Enzo away.

The driver hopped back on his bike and Enzo shouted after him, "If I find out you are involved or touched her, you are a dead man! I will find out and I will be coming for you!"

A moment of exhausted silence passed between Enzo and Vito.

Vito's mind raced. *What is this about? Who is Enzo really? Why did I let Teresa talk me into coming here? Why did I put my little Lulu into this situation?* The repetition went on and on.

To their surprise, Giovanni and Peter came stumbling in to sight. The older of the two placed his hand on Vito's shoulder. "No worries," Peter said. "Laura will be okay. Teresa told me she is nearby, alive and safe. I am quiet, but I observe it all . . . That crazy sister-in-law has been coming around. You should have counted on that, Vito. She thinks I don't see what she is doing, but I watch her, and she is a fool. Once your plans were made, she made her presence known. I see her talking to Vincenzo too much. Put two and two together; there is no other reason for her to be in these parts. We know people in other parts. She is no good. They talk of her and the innocence of your brother. Vincenzo is no good, just no good. I just sit back, let it be, and just wait. I know Teresa is watching over us and she was no fool. Let's go north. Something smells in the north."

The four men staggered into the truck as they lacked any other formal plan. Enzo drove; Vito, bleary-eyed and exhausted, sat beside him. As soon as he had his Laura back, Vito decided he and his daughter would be on the first train back to Rome and the first flight back to their home in America.

As if reading Vito's mind, Peter said, "Enzo is no fool. Give him a chance, Vito. I know how you are feeling."

Giovanni added, "He is a good man, Vito. Try to see this. If Maria is involved, he will get to the bottom of it."

Vito's head dropped as he moaned and made the sign of the cross. He knew what this all meant for him. He did not want to do this. Once again, his worst nightmare had come to pass.

He had to find and face Maria, once and for all. Hearing what Peter had to say, it was pretty evident to him that Maria must have had something to do with this. Would he be able to control his life-long urge to kill his brother's wife, and had she ever fessed up to Dominick about all the evil she had committed against him and his baby daughter? Had she let Dominick live with the lie that the baby they had supposedly adopted really had died?

Once Vito had gotten word all those years ago that Ana was alive and would be returned to him, he had vowed that he would never return to Italy and never speak of this to his brother. He vowed not to let one more person suffer from Maria's actions and just let them live in peace as his way to show gratitude for her safe return. He had kept his word until now, but the demons inside him never slept much.

⊙⌖⊙

The next morning, Laura stirred in the strange bed. She kept thinking about the crazy things Maria had told her. Could Ana really be only her half-sister? From their looks to their age gap, she assessed their differences. Was her father really married before? None of this had ever been spoken about in her family. It all seemed impossible. She wanted her mother. She wanted to go home. But her thoughts kept leading her back to Enzo. As she tried to process what was going on, she kept hearing his words, seeing his face, and melting into his eyes. She thought of her poor pop, who must have been distraught by now. She could not justify to herself or even understand her erratic behavior these past few days.

Alfonso had promised he would return her to Enzo's home, but Laura now knew that was a lie. She was trapped and the door was securely locked. She had no idea what was planned for her. What could they all have against her?

Light now streamed into the room from the single, small window. Laura got up and pulled aside the curtain. She gasped at the scenery, which had been masked in darkness the night before. The Sicilian countryside sprawled before her, sparkling in the morning light.

Once Laura got out of bed, she suddenly realized that her period had arrived overnight. She had been a late bloomer as compared to most of her friends. She did not get her menses until she was at the tail end of her fifteenth year. This was still an unfamiliar event in her life. Almost a nonevent. No acne, no cramps, no erratic behaviors, or mood swings. Basically seamless.

But when Teresa passed, her menses had ceased. Caterina was concerned about this, but had attributed this to her suffering through the emotional loss of Teresa. Laura actually laughed when she saw the early morning arrival. She finally connected the dots and realized that this had to be the reason for all of her unfamiliar thoughts, behaviors, and terrible back pain.

She paused for a moment and thought it fitting that, upon arriving in Italy, meeting Enzo, and reading Teresa's letter, she was finally able to let go of the grief she was holding deep within. Her body was letting go, and all was coming full circle. She thought how this would go over when she explained all of her recent actions to her father.

"So, pop, I was temporarily insane, you see, for a few days because I got my period back again."

How could she ever utter these words to him, she wondered? She felt horrible for putting him through this and was sure that by now he wanted to kill her. Oh, then there was Enzo. How would she explain this all to him?

Luckily for Laura, she was imprisoned in a girl's room. It was well stocked with all the supplies she could ever possibly need. So all of her personal requirements were met. She couldn't imagine trying to explain this to anyone or asking for necessary supplies for this unwelcomed event, much less in Italian.

Chapter Twelve

Vito spilled out of the cab of the truck, the bright sunlight of early morning bearing down on his scowling face. He acknowledged Peter and Giovanni's departure with a single curt nod, then marched to the front door of the house and knocked powerfully. His scowl deepened as the sound of muffled chatter greeted him from beyond the door. After a moment, the door opened a crack. There was a gasp and a loud exclamation from within the house, and the door was thrown open.

An enormous man stood framed in the doorway, his eyes wide with shock. He was the spitting image of Vito.

They regarded each other for a minute, this man and Vito, neither wanting to make the first move. Something shifted in both men in the same instant, and they collapsed into each other, sobbing and laughing and unable to let the other go too quickly.

"You got fat, big brother," the man said with a grin.

"I'm American now, Dominick," Vito responded, "and you are rather thick yourself!"

They separated reluctantly, smiling.

"We weren't expecting to see you this early," Dominick said. "Why, Vito? Why have you stayed away so long? You and me, we are all that is left of our family. We should be together. This will always be your home. I've missed you terribly."

"We're here to get Laura," Vito replied, the smile falling away from his face.

Dominick frowned in confusion. "Laura?"

Vito paled. "She's not here?" he asked in a whisper. His emotions were unstable.

Dominick shook his head. "Vito, what are you saying?' he asked, an edge of fear creeping into his voice. "I can't wait to meet my niece. It is so wrong that you have never brought your children here. That we have never met."

Vito felt frozen solid.

❦

Laura stood at the window and mused. From beyond the closed door, she heard shuffling and muffled whispers. She stood in front of the door, steeled herself, and tried to force it open. The door wouldn't budge.

A gaggle of Russo women stood in the hallway outside. They hummed with excited energy, giggling at Laura's attempts to get out. Alfonso's mother, Sarah, stepped forward and unlocked the door. The women shrieked with delight at the sight of Laura, standing wide-eyed in the doorway. Laura jumped at the noise, and the women howled with laughter.

Sarah separated herself from the crowd. She hugged Laura, kissing her enthusiastically on each cheek. "Laura, you are a beautiful girl," she said between kisses, "welcome to our home! We are so happy to meet you and to have you here! If there's anything at all that you need today, you let anyone here know and we'll get it for you right away. How does that sound?"

Laura blinked at her, the foreign language rolling over her like a wave. Sarah looked at her blankly, smiling. The women looked at Laura expectantly, and Laura felt a swell of panic rise within her.

"I don't speak Italian too well," Laura said with a shrug. "I need to leave. Alfonso promised me he would return me to Partanna, to my father."

Sarah stared at her, stunned. After a moment of silence, the other women erupted into laughter. Laura turned beet red, her panic escalating.

Sarah regarded Laura for a moment, shaking her head and looking a little overwhelmed. "Well," she continued in Italian, "you are welcome into my home all the same, Laura."

She enveloped Laura in a big hug. All at once, the other women descended on Laura, hugging and kissing her and laughing infectiously. Laura couldn't help but start to smile, just for a moment.

"Come on," Sarah said, tugging on her hand. "We've got breakfast waiting for you."

Unsure of her destination but certain the women meant her no harm, Laura allowed herself to be herded into the hallway. They took her to the dining room where a long wooden table sat overflowing with a feast of breakfast foods. They seated Laura at the head of the table and passed her enormous plates of food.

A young she girl gave Laura a wreath of flowers to put in her hair. Laura stared at the wreath for a breath; it was made entirely of small white olive flowers.

"Fiord d'oliva," Laura whispered to herself. She smiled, feeling a bit like a character in a movie, and placed the wreath on her head.

⊙Ɣ⊙

Vito, Enzo, and Dominick sat around a small round wooden table on Dominick's terrace. Expansive farmland stretched behind them, waves of gold and green spreading on for miles. Dominick had increased the farm and made a beautiful vineyard. His home was impressive. The beauty of the scenery was lost on Vito, whose distress increased with each passing minute. His discomfort was as intense as it had been the day he found out Maria was behind Ana's disappearance.

"Where could she be, Dominick?" he groaned, leaning back in his chair to bury his face in his hands. "Please, think!"

Dominick spread his hands, his face pained. "I don't know, Vito.

I just don't know. I've considered every possibility, but I just . . . was she unhappy about Enzo? She must have wanted to escape that situation." His voice trailed away, and the men sat in silence, thinking.

The patio door suddenly opened, and Maria stood in the doorway, her expression a mixture of veiled triumph and exasperation. For Vito, the dreaded moment had just arrived.

"Are you looking for Laura?" she asked, her lips curling in a cruel smile. "Is that what this is all about?"

Vito's head slowly rose, and he fixed Maria with a threatening stare. "Do you know where she is?"

"I do," she responded. She pointed an accusatory finger at Enzo. "She came to me last night begging for my help to free her from you and this man, I suppose. She's getting married. This time, Vito, we are doing it my way. The next time you see her she will properly suited and married."

❦

Stuffed and at ease, Laura refused more plates of food thrust at her by the smiling women. She tried to help clear the table, but the women surrounded her and ushered her deeper into the house. Laura's unease, which had subsided over the course of the meal, began to reappear, but she resisted the urge to struggle free and dash from the house.

The throng of women turned a corner in the hallway and entered a large sitting room. Laura gasped at the sight. Every surface—couches, tables, bookshelves—was covered with frilly white lace, huge snowy skirts, and puffy satin sleeves.

Wedding dresses. Dozens of them.

Laura felt her face go utterly pale.

❦

The three men sat in stunned silence, staring at Maria. Vito looked outraged; Dominick looked stunned. Enzo, however, looked unconvinced.

After a long moment, Enzo asked, "To whom?"

"I'm surprised," Maria replied coolly. "I thought you would be more upset."

Enzo repeated his question, "To whom?"

Maria sized him up and rolled her eyes. "That," she said with a sly smile, "I'm not going to tell you."

Very slowly, Vito rose from his chair. He took a menacing step forward, and Dominick instantly got to his feet, ready to jump. "Maria," Vito said, his voice almost a snarl, "where is my daughter?"

Maria's response was a silent, condescending grin. Enraged, Vito grabbed the day-old loaf of Italian bread from the table and slapped it against his open palm. Maria rolled her eyes, and Vito brandished the loaf like a sword, pointing it at her face.

"Where is my daughter?" he demanded.

Maria gave him a withering look. "She's fine, Vito."

"Where is my daughter?"

"I'm not going to tell you."

Vito lurched forward, shoving his crimson face into Maria's face and quivering with rage. When he spoke, his voice was deadly. "She. Is. Not. Getting. Married. You got that, Maria? You will be dead before I ever let that happen. You will never win. Not again, not as long as I am alive."

Maria shrugged as a smirk played across her lips. "Looks like you forgot what it means to be a Baccaro, Vito."

Vito snapped. Howling in rage, he lunged at Maria, but Dominick was a second ahead of his brother and took the brunt of the blow. Enzo leapt to his feet and helped Dominick wrestle Vito away from Maria. They shoved Vito into a chair, pinning him by the shoulders.

"Where is my daughter?!" Vito roared, his hands grasping in the air in search of Maria's throat.

"Vito, my brother," Dominick cried, "what is all this about? Maria means no harm! She is a good woman. Please do not speak to my beautiful wife this way. She has only good intentions."

Vito stared at Dominick in disbelief, his jaw going slack. His arms fell limply onto the arms of the chair. "Are you blind, Dominick?" he begged in a pained whisper. "How is it that you cannot see what I see? How can you possibly not know all there is to know?"

"Vito," Maria interjected, her voice cold, "if you had any Italian blood left in you, you would understand the favor I am doing for this family."

"My Italian blood is doing just fine, thank you!" Vito snapped. "Be clear that my blood is NOT your blood. My children are NOT your children, nor do you share any blood with us. You never have and never will." Vito was astounded to find that the tenacity of this woman has not yet paled. She still had no fear, and no worries about being exposed to Dominick. Her secret had never been exposed to him. Vito was amazed.

"What kind of Italian abandons their family, Vito?" Maria demanded, her voice becoming shrill. "For over thirty years you disappeared, and the only reason you came back was to marry your daughter off to someone from *Partanna*?!" She turned and spat at Enzo.

"She didn't come here to marry me!" Enzo fired back.

"You're right," Maria said with false cheer. "Because she respects her family. Because she came to marry into her own family's heritage, into my town, which should have been her town! She came here because she wishes to be among the women who should have been her sisters, to see the family Vito refused to share with her! No, Vito took that opportunity from us, too—the opportunity to love her as her family has a right to!" She turned to Vito, the false calm evaporating from her face. "It should be your family that receives your fat, American money, Vito. Not some stranger. Not some stranger from *Partanna*." She spat the word *Partanna* as if the word alone was revolting to her. "You have no idea what a disgrace I'm saving you from, Vito. What a disgrace I'm saving this family from."

Vito let out a short, humorless bark of a laugh. "My daughter is being married off to save your pride? You are as crazy as ever." He turned to his brother, his eyes filling with tears. "Dom, this is why I haven't seen you in thirty goddamned years. I could have had her killed back then, but I didn't because of my love for you, Dom. That may have been my biggest mistake yet. I now know it should have been done long ago."

Dominick looked stunned, clueless as to the true source of Vito's anger. Vito watched as several emotions worked over his brother's face—hurt, dismay, confusion, even anger—and it confirmed to him that Dominick had no idea of what kind of woman Maria really was. "Your daughter, she asks my Maria for help," Dominick said. "Maria is a good woman, and she will help her. Remember we have no children. She just wants to be involved. We lost our baby long ago, so she tries maybe a bit too much. But she is so good. I love you, Vito, but you come into my home to disrespect us and say you want to kill my wife? I do not understand?"

Maria stood over him with a look on her face that said she'd have liked very much to spit on him or kick dirt in his face. "At least I *have* my pride, Vito," she said, quietly. "You have nothing. Your daughter tells me you try to control her. Just like you tried to control me and your other daughter years ago. This is why she left you last night. She is happy now. She told me so."

She turned on her heel and walked into the house. The men watched her leave, their faces frozen in expressions of shock.

Dominick looked pleadingly at Vito, but he could offer nothing to comfort his brother. He firmly believed what Maria had said. Vito's heart went out to him, knowing Dominick knew nothing of the truth. He was a good soul, but when it came to his wife, he was spineless and clueless. Vito spared him the truth.

It would break his heart, Vito thought, *or worse, he might not even believe the truth. It's easier to stay far, far away. I should never have left New York; I should never have brought Laura here.*

At the thought of Laura, possibly lost and afraid, his heart broke again, and he hung his head as tears began to stream down his face. He could not believe that Maria had been able to interfere in his life for a second time, and yet this time with his precious Laura. That she still could exist all these years living with the evil and secrets of the past and still reach out to manipulate in such deceitful ways was something that Vito struggled with. He was not able to get past this for the life of him.

Laura struggled in vain against the dozens of hands that tugged her about, pulling and fussing and trying to force gown after lacy gown over her head. The women weren't malicious, but they were persistent and they mistook her resistance for shyness.

Eventually, one of them succeeded and managed to force a gigantic lacy mess of a gown onto Laura's slender frame. The gaggle guffawed, lovingly mocking the older woman for having such a big gown, then pulled the gown off Laura and forced another one on before she could protest.

Laura felt agitated that so many strangers were touching her. She tried a final time to squirm out of the onslaught of dresses, but to no avail. Unable to think of any other way to communicate, she steeled herself, mustered her determination . . . and forced herself into dramatic, gulping sobs.

The women's actions came to an instantaneous halt. They gasped in dismay at her breakdown, cooing and trying to comfort her, but Laura refused to calm down. Sarah stepped forward, swept her arms around Laura and hurried her out of the room, keeping herself between Laura and the other women who came rushing in her wake. She ushered Laura into the bedroom and slammed the door in the others' faces.

Laura collapsed onto the bed and buried her face in her hands. She tried to gain control, but the fake tears had led to real ones and she gasped for breath. Sarah sat next to her and stroked her back. Laura could tell by the amused look on her face that Sarah had misinterpreted her sobbing.

"I . . . I don't . . . want . . . " Laura choked out between gasps.

"Ssssh, it's okay," Sarah soothed in Italian. Laura suddenly wanted to wring her neck. "We'll let you rest now. This dress, I think it's the one, don't you?"

Laura was incapable of understanding a word Sarah said, so Sarah rose to leave. Laura sat up immediately, nearly swamped by satin and lace, and clutched at her hand, desperate to make her understand.

"Sarah! Please, I don't want . . . " She waved her hands frantically at the wedding dress, shaking her head violently. "Not for me! No wedding! Please, please let me go find my father!"

Sarah smiled. "You're right," she said. "I think the other dress was better."

She kissed the top of Laura's head and left the room, beaming. Laura stared at the closed door, stunned; surely Sarah understood panic when she saw it?

Laura realized suddenly that it was hopeless; she would never be able to communicate with Sarah. In that moment, determination overtook her fear.

"I will not marry Alfonso," she whispered to herself. "I will get out of here, and I will see my father again . . . I'll see Enzo again."

She rose from the bed, her eyes finally dry, and hurried to the window, but it was extremely small and there was no way for her to climb through. She peered out at the sky, and warmth flooded her chest.

"*Le nuvole sono belle,*" she said, smiling to herself. *The clouds are beautiful.*

She left the window and tiptoed to the door, pressing her ear against the wood to listen for a moment. Convinced it was quiet outside her room, she shimmied out of the wedding dress and tried the door. Her heart leapt as it opened a crack; they'd forgotten to lock her in.

It must be my lucky day, she thought as she slipped silently out into the hallway.

❧

Vito charged out of Dominick's house, slamming the door behind him. He cracked his knuckles as if bracing for a fight, his face crimson with rage.

Enzo came sprinting after him, desperate to catch up. "Please, let me come with you!" he pleaded.

"I've had enough of your help for a lifetime, Enzo," Vito said painfully, his face had thunderous scowl.

"We'll cover twice as much ground together," Enzo insisted.

"I don't want that woman to leave your sight. She has something up her sleeve." Vito shouted in his face, jabbing his finger at the house.

"I know people in this town," Enzo begged. "I can—"

Vito grabbed Enzo by the front of his shirt, nearly lifting him off the ground. His eyes blazed, reminding Enzo suddenly—painfully—of Laura's angry eyes.

"This is your fault, Enzo," Vito said, his voice low, dangerous, and matter-of-fact. Enzo's stomach dropped. "You write of love to my baby girl, convinced Teresa—God rest her soul—that you and my Lulu are meant to be, and then you scare her with your manly attentions! She is just a little girl!" Vito paused, studying the look of guilt Enzo knew had spread instantly over his face. "So when I tell you to stay put, you stay put. You left her last night, and that should have never been. Do what I tell you to do now. That woman needs to be watched. I need to be far away from her."

"I want to help," Enzo said in a pleading whisper.

"This isn't your fight," Vito spat. "You have no claim on Laura."

"I just—"

"The second I find Laura," Vito snapped, cutting him off, "I'm taking her to back New York. She's not marrying someone from this God-forsaken place, and she sure as hell isn't marrying you."

He released Enzo, and Enzo staggered back. Vito turned on his heel and stormed off down the road. Enzo watched him as he made his way to the nearest house, which stood in the distance, red dust swirling in his wake in the hot sun.

Realizing Vito was not coming back for him, Enzo turned and slumped obediently back toward the house. He tried not to believe that any of what Maria had said was true. He felt responsible, worried, frustrated, and understanding of Vito's outbursts toward him all at the same time.

Chapter Thirteen

Wearing only her white slip, Laura tiptoed down the hallway. Peals of laughter and conversation wafted toward her from the back of the house, so she slunk the other way, her heart pounding. She opened the front door a crack, peeped out, and then stepped out onto the terrace. Her bare feet made no noise on the ground as she snuck away from the house.

As she passed a scrawny tree that stood in the yard, Vincenzo, the tall, burly mobster, suddenly emerged. Laura didn't see him, but continued her skulking across the grass, sure she hadn't been spotted. Vincenzo's face cracked in a smile, and followed her for a few steps before clearing his throat.

At the sound, Laura leapt like she'd been scalded and whirled to face him. He stood almost a foot taller than she and was nearly twice as broad.

"Where are you going, little bride-to-be?" he asked, his tone conversational.

Laura, momentarily thrown off by his use of English, drew herself up, glaring firmly at him as if to pierce him with her eyes. "I'm going home," she informed him flatly.

Vincenzo chuckled. "This is your home now," he said, pointing nonchalantly over his shoulder toward the Russo house.

Laura clenched her jaw and shook her head. "Alfonso said . . ."

Her voice wavered as Vincenzo raised an eyebrow, and she silently cursed herself. "He said I can go anywhere. Whatever I want. He said he would take me home today. I am free to go."

Vincenzo put his hand on the small of her back and began to guide her back to the house. "That's interesting," he said cheerfully, "because he told me you were going to try to run away."

Laura slipped under his arm and began to walk briskly away. Vincenzo rolled his eyes and jogged after her. He reached out to grab her shoulder, and she slapped his hand away, anger burning in her eyes.

"I'll scream," she threatened. "You touch me, I will scream so loud. And everyone will see you hurt me. You are going to be sorry you did this once my father finds out."

Vincenzo laughed, a full, hearty guffaw, and Laura used his distraction as an opportunity to bolt. She took off at a wild dash. From behind, she heard Vincenzo let out a loud, piercing whistle. She glanced over her shoulder to see ten or so Vincenzo-sized gangsters emerge from the house and the backyard like lions from a den.

They overtook her in an instant, and she panicked, flailing her arms, kicking and scratching. She punched one man in the jaw and kneed another in the gut, managing to break away and dash several yards further. One man overtook her in two bounds, grabbing her arm and twisting it violently behind her, knocking her to the ground. They immediately formed a perimeter around her, and guns she hadn't noticed before flashed from several waistlines and coat pockets.

Laura's blood ran cold, but anger boiled up again from the pit of her stomach. She quickly got to her feet, panting, and stood straight, her jaw clenched in defiance.

Vincenzo entered the little circle. He wasn't smiling now; he looked annoyed and unimpressed.

"Trust me," Vincenzo said, "you're lucky you're ending up with Alfonso."

He slid his hand around her waist, pulled her into him until her chin rested on his chest. Laura put her hands up, mimicking Enzo's mannerism. The men chuckled, and Laura realized she was in over her head. Terror started to set in. She felt her father's intense pain and worry at not knowing where she was at this moment.

Shoving Vincenzo away, Laura turned on her heels and pushed through the wall of thugs. She walked slowly and determinedly to the front door of the house, slamming it behind her as she reentered the building. One of the thugs, Italo, let out a low whistle.

"Alfonso's in for one hell of a wedding night," he said.

The men cackled and sauntered after her into the house, hauling her back to the bedroom. They locked her in again, but terror had given away to cold, calculating hatred.

They'll pay for this. All of them.

⚜

Vincenzo felt that there was too much at stake; this job was paying a lot of money. He knew Laura was a flight risk. He called a meeting with the Russo men, and together they agreed that for the time being she needed to be moved.

But this time, Vincenzo decided, the manner in which they did so was going to have more impact than the cavalier manner in which Antonio had delivered her in. Vincenzo told the others he'd take care of the details. Being the twisted soul that he was, he went to Laura's room with cloth, lots of cloth.

Without a word he grabbed her, covered her eyes, gagged her, and tied her wrists together. Laura struggled, truly fearing for her life. Vincenzo knew she was scared out of her mind, and now he could make the impact he felt was so important to ensure this plan would move forward. He snuck Laura out of the house, ensuring that none of the woman would notice and try to stop him. He placed her in his truck, still struggling.

He drove for miles and finally found the old abandoned freight car he used on occasion to store his stolen goods.

Laura's heart pounded, wondering if Vincenzo was going to kill her, rape her, or abandon her. She couldn't control the whimpering.

She chided herself for having left the room and wondered where all the ladies had been when Vincenzo was forcibly removing her from the home. She figured the thug had arranged to slip her out without their noticing.

Vincenzo locked her in a large cage of some sort, but first removed the gag and blindfold, keeping her hands loosely bound. The accommodations were dank, dark, and depressing. He lit a candle, which provided some dim lighting. Now he sat in front of her and would not speak. She tried and tried to get through to him. First she shouted, then she tried using a soft voice. Nothing worked.

After a while, he provided her with a little food and water. At one point, she had to relieve herself in a rather demeaning way. Although he hadn't touched her in any suggestive way, she was surely frightened of what he would do. When he dozed, she tried to find a way out of her prison, but to her disappointment, the lock was solid and the bars wouldn't budge.

When he awoke, he seemed different, softer in a way. He finally spoke, using his best English, so that she would understand. "Look, I really am not here to hurt you. But you have to accept that you are going to marry Alfonso. He is not so bad, okay, a bit small, but not a bad guy. You will do okay with him."

"But I don't know him," Laura pleaded. "I don't love him. I didn't come here for this."

He remained silent. It seemed like hours had passed in silence before they both dozed off. In the dark freight car, there was no telling what time of day or night it was. A while later, they awoke.

Vincenzo perked up a bit and asked, "So why did you come here? I hear you came to Italy for someone else? What is the difference?"

Laura missed Enzo so much at this point. "I cannot put it into words," she replied. "It is a feeling. It is his touch, and it is his heart. He is rare, and he is good. I realize that even more so now. Being forced to marry someone else makes my heart see what my heart really wants. It is not Alfonso."

Time passed.

"Who is he?" Vincenzo finally asked.

Laura did not answer. She simply asked instead, "Do you love, do you have that feeling for anyone?"

More time passed.

"I do, but I am invisible to her," he said breaking the silence.

Laura gave a weak smile. "Maybe it is your line of work," she suggested. "Maybe if you changed and worked at being honorable, she would notice you. Why do you want to do this? It is so wrong. Don't you want to be a father one day? How will your children ever respect you? . . . What is her name?"

Silence.

After what seemed like a painful uncomfortable eternity, Vincenzo replied, "Soph."

Laura perked up. "What?"

More silence.

Laura mused over the coincidence. *Could it be the same one—Enzo's friend?*

Vincenzo added, "She is beautiful, but she would never be with me. This would not be the life for her. But I wonder and think all the time. She has a thing for this oil man."

Laura's heart dropped, realizing whom he meant. But then she said softly, "Just try, listen to your heart. When you are good, good things will come."

"I don't know, I just don't know anymore. I am sorry about you and Alfonso. I know you will break the other guy's heart. But I have to do this. There is no way out for either of us."

Laura whispered, "There is always a way out."

⟊⟊⟊

Enzo anxiously paced the floor, oblivious to Maria's growing irritation. She tapped her fingers and sighed pointedly at Enzo.

"You really should leave here, Partanna boy," she sniped. "You're not welcome in this house. You're not welcome in this *town!*"

"I'm not going anywhere," Enzo replied, raising his voice. "I'm not going anywhere until Laura is safe."

"That is not your business. Your little American sweetheart is not interested in you. She told me so last night," Maria said. "She stood at my door, begging me to help her . . . to save her from the likes of you. She wants a good Italian man from a stable family. You have nothing to offer her."

"You're lying," Enzo said, but his mind had begun racing despite his outward disbelief. "What you offer to this family is disgusting," he raged. "You are a disgrace."

Maria smugly turned her back on him. She had seen the doubt spread across his features. Her plan would move ahead just fine. It had to. She had plotted for thirty years to seek her revenge on Vito. Any man who would keep his children from family, especially from those who can't bear children, is cruel. Those with children must share them, not hide them in the far corners of another country. This is what Maria truly believed.

It could have been twenty-four hours or forty-eight. Laura lost all sense of time in her cage in the dirty, old freight train. But what she did remember was Vincenzo tying her hands and covering her eyes once again and loading her into the car. It seemed to be nighttime. He, again, would not speak.

They drove and drove, and she was concerned about their destination. Some time later, she was finally returned to the room at Alfonso's house that had been her holding cell. No one was awake and no one greeted her. He deposited her, locked the door behind him, but before he did, he said, "I had to do this. Forget the other guy and live a happy life with Alfonso. We all have our crosses to bear." *Click.*

Laura paced the bedroom floor, her mind working. As she passed the window for the dozenth time, a flash of copper caught her eye and she bent down to study it. A shiny American penny lay on the ground. She picked it up curiously and scrutinized the date.

1925? She searched her memory for the significance of the year, and a chill ran up her spine. *The year Enzo was born.*

She stood bolt upright, an idea rippled through her like an electric current. She was so tired and ached for the comfort of a real bed and immediately decided she needed to rest. She tried to beckon sleep, but her mind was in overdrive. *The penny, that penny,* she thought, as sleep finally claimed her, *Enzo, Enzo, hmm what would Enzo do?*

Upon wakening, she raced to the door and called for Sarah. An idea had come to her that night. Sarah was thrilled to have her future daughter in law back in her clutches.

Within minutes, Laura came bustling into the Russo family kitchen. The gaggle of women that bustled around the space were hard at work cooking what looked like a feast for hundreds when Laura burst in on the chaotic scene. She kept her head high and face glowing, trying to play the part of the excited bride as best she could. The women halted as she entered. "Oh, Laura, we missed you so! Welcome back!"

"I need olive oil," she cried.

They stared at her, confused. After a lengthy, surprised pause, one of the little girls scurried to the table, picked up a bottle of olive oil and handed it cautiously to Laura. The women tried to suppress giggles.

Laura nodded eagerly, pointing to the bottle and looking Sarah firmly in the eye. "No. I need a lot of olive oil. I need a bathtub of olive oil."

She pointed to the bottle, threw her hands in a wide circle, and mimicked washing her hair. She repeated the charade until, eventually, understanding and amusement bloomed on Sarah's face. She turned and chattered to the women, who burst into hysterical laughter.

Laura stared at the incredulous group of women and repeated her mime, her face as serious as she could make it. The laughter gave way to frowns and murmurs. "Does the American girl know some secret about soaking in olive oil before one's wedding or is this an American remedy to reduce cramping?" they seemed to be asking.

Laura made it seem so.

Enzo paced the house, growing more frantic and hopeless by the minute. Maria was somewhere else in the house, out of sight, but her presence—a hot cup of coffee on the table, an open book—lingered.

Hours had passed since he'd spoken with Vito, and Laura's father's oath lingered in his mind. *She sure as hell isn't going to marry you!*

Enzo shook his head to clear his anxiety, but all the action did was make him dizzy.

As his head spun, a frantic pounding sounded on the door. Enzo leapt to open the door, an expectant smile on his face. The smile instantly fell at the sight of Italo, a muscular but simple-minded thug, standing on the doorstep. The two regarded each other for a moment, both clearly bewildered by the other's presence.

"I need to speak to Maria," Italo said finally.

"She's out," Enzo lied.

"Okay," Italo said. "You're the perfect guy. You could help me. Is your delivery truck nearby?"

Enzo scowled. "Why?"

"Well, I can't say," Italo said. "But actually I don't even understand why, but we need a lot of olive oil."

"I'm not going to let you drive my truck," Enzo replied. Enzo protected that truck as if it were his own.

"No, I . . . do you have olive oil with you?" Italo asked.

Enzo struggled against the urge to roll his eyes. "Does it look like I have olive oil with me?"

Italo gave him a patient look, as if Enzo were stupid. "What else would you be doing here?"

"What *are* you doing here?"

"I'm getting oil."

"From me?"

"If you got it."

Enzo shook his head. "Then why come to Maria's house?"

"You're killing me, Enzo."

"I'm not giving you oil if I don't know why," Enzo replied, incapable of keeping the sarcasm out of his voice. "Why suddenly do you need oil? You work at the flour factory, right? At least, that's what your mother *thinks* you do."

"Okay, fine," Italo conceded. "Alfonso Russo's getting married to some American girl who said she needed to take a bath in olive oil first. So, we need oil. From you or someone like you."

Enzo's mouth fell open, and hope rose in his chest. "What?"

Italo, his chest swelling with pride at the thought of knowing something Enzo didn't, explained, "Over in America, Italian brides bathe in olive oil before the wedding. I bet it makes them slippery on their wedding night, you know?"

Enzo raised an incredulous eyebrow at Italo, who chortled at his own joke. Frantic for more information, Enzo struggled to keep his voice calm and detached, not wanting to look too eager. "Well, first, what does Maria have to do with this? How much do you need, and I need to know who is paying for the oil?" he asked, trying to keep this as though it was a regular business transaction.

"Enough to fill a bathtub," Italo replied, holding up his hand and ticking off one finger at a time as if he'd kept a checklist in his head. "At Alfonso's house. Don't worry, Enzo, you will get paid. And it is Maria's favorite niece; that's how she's involved. I think she will pay for the olive oil." He quickly gave Enzo explicit directions to where the delivery needed to be made.

Enzo stood nailed to the floor for a moment, his chin on his hand as if considering whether the trip would be worth his while. Italo shuffled from foot to foot in growing agitation.

"Wedding's in six hours," the thug finally said, "so get going."

"I'll be there," Enzo replied coolly. His mind was racing. Italo sized Enzo up warily, not sure he could trust him, but he finally shrugged and sauntered off. As soon as he was out of sight, Enzo dashed to his truck.

He was willing to pay his boss for the oil, but pressing Italo for that information gave him more insight into this situation. *Maria is pure evil. How did she become this way?* he wondered. Checking on Maria one more time, he saw that she was snoring in a chair, and Enzo departed in a quiet manner. Dominick was nowhere to be found.

Laura stood in the kitchen, surrounded by Sarah and the other women. In her hands she held an old stained cookbook. She flipped through the worn pages, each recipe scrawled in different handwriting. With each turn of the page, she paused, shook her head, looked at the waiting group of women, looked back at the book, and kept flipping. Their anticipation grew palpably with each turn of the page. She flipped another page and her eyes lit up.

"This one," she said, tapping her finger on the page. "Chicken Masala."

The women applauded eagerly at the recipe selection and began bustling around, assembling ingredients and tools. Sarah led Laura to the sink to wash her hands. The soap dish was empty, and Sarah had to scrounge under the sink for a new bar. She handed it to Laura, and Laura's eyes went wide.

The bar was wrapped in crimson paper, the package closed with a piece of twine. Laura sniffed it and smiled. *"Insaponare,"* she said, and Sarah beamed.

Laura washed her hands and turned back to the kitchen full of eager women. As the last traces of the scent of the soap lingered about, Laura felt Teresa's presence in the room, and a sense of comfort washed over her.

Enzo's truck careened to a stop, dust billowing in its wake. Enzo looked up at the house, steeling himself. He kept his eyes open for any sign of Vito, Peter, and Giovanni, who were also on foot, but they too were nowhere to be found. Italo came out of the front door, and Enzo slid out of the truck. He circled to the back and opened the gate. Several vats of olive oil stood waiting in the bed of the vehicle. Enzo's truck was always loaded with enough oil for two days' worth of deliveries; he had more than enough oil to fill a bathtub.

Together, Enzo and Italo unloaded several drums of oil, hauling them into the house.

As Enzo emptied the truck bed of the drums, he silently thanked God for his employer, a decent man who valued Enzo's loyalty to him. He felt so blessed to be trusted with his truck and multiple day's supply of oil. Having this in his possession could possibly help save Laura, he hoped.

⌖

The Russo kitchen was filled with steam, the smell of spices, and the animated chatter of the women. Laura was trying to mimic Sarah's technique of cutting a tomato into perfect squares; several butchered tomatoes laid discarded on the cutting board. Suddenly, she heard the front door slam shut. Italo's and Enzo's voices wafted into the kitchen from the hallway.

Laura's back went ramrod straight at the sound of Enzo's voice. Though she couldn't understand what was being said, the knowledge of his presence made her feel instantly safer. Something else, a new sensation, flooded through her chest just as relief flooded her mind, and she shoved the sensation away.

"You want the oil in the kitchen?" Enzo asked loudly from the hallway.

"No, no," Sarah called back. The "no, no" was all Laura could understand. "In the bathroom . . . Enzo! Here, Enzo."

Enzo sauntered into the kitchen, the vat looked light in his arms. Laura and Enzo instantly locked eyes, and Laura felt a surge of energy course between them. It took all of her will not to cry out his name and run into his arms.

Sarah noticed the exchange and raised an eyebrow. "I guess it's bath time," she said, nailing Enzo with a stare. "Are you ready, Laura, or does the oil need to sit a bit?"

Enzo tore his eyes away from Laura and trotted out of the room. Laura suppressed a sigh of relief; he now knew where she was, and he knew she was safe. A sense of peace came over her, mingled with another, deeper, stronger emotion. His eyes had said all that needed to be said.

Laura steeled herself and allowed Sarah to escort her away from the cutting board and into the hall. She did her best to keep her expression neutral.

A grumpy Italo passed them in the hallway, having already brought two heavy drums of oil to the bathroom. Enzo seemed amused by Italo's huffiness; he called after him in a decidedly mocking tone. The humor in his voice made Laura's heart beat faster. She entered the bathroom, breathless, struggling to keep her face neutral. Enzo's smile fell away, and he and Laura tried desperately not to stare at each other. Sarah left the room for a moment, closing the door behind her, and Laura seized her chance.

"Enzo, I'm helpless here," she said in a fierce whisper. "My father —my poor papa—he must be crazy by now! I am so sorry for everything. Please forgive me!"

Enzo could see she was unharmed but still asked, "Have they hurt you here?"

The door flew open and Sarah stalked in, carrying a bathrobe. She glared at Enzo and ushered him out. He threw a parting look of desperation at Laura as Sarah closed the door in his face. She turned to Laura, smiling. Laura turned to the bright green olive oil in the tub and her heart sank.

Oh, boy. I have really done it now, she said silently.

Enzo stalked through the house until he located Vincenzo. His reaction to this insanity incensed him. The thug stood in the center of the wedding dress–strewn sitting room, and he greeted Enzo with a condescending smirk.

"There's been a mistake," Enzo said flatly. As he surveyed the surroundings, an idea was slowly forming in his mind.

"Not my problem," Vincenzo replied coolly, turning his face dismissively away.

Enzo scowled. "The American girl didn't come here to marry Alfonso."

Vincenzo rolled his eyes and returned his gaze to Enzo. "And I suppose she came to marry you?" Vincenzo had no clue about Enzo and Laura's long-distance romance. He didn't concern himself with the idle gossip that went around the town.

For a moment, Enzo was flabbergasted. He quickly regained his composure, setting his jaw defiantly and refusing to answer. Vincenzo laughed, low and menacing. He flipped the hem of his jacket back to rest a hand on his hip, giving Enzo a deliberately clear view of the now-familiar gun in his pants pocket.

"Get out of here," Vincenzo ordered. "You don't even know her and you are trying to save the day. Deliver your oil and go. Mind your damn business."

"Vincenzo," Enzo replied, keeping his voice calm and unpleading, "I could have burned you so many times, and I never did. I never worked for you, but I kept my mouth shut. I've covered for you, even when it was the last thing I wanted to do. When will you ever see this?"

"Leave," Vincenzo replied.

"Just let the girl go," Enzo demanded. "You quarrel is with me, not with her."

Vincenzo scoffed. "Do I look like I care?" he said, smiling broadly. "I still owe you for the morning water trick, you bastard. If my mother hadn't been there, you wouldn't be here now. As far as I'm concerned, the war between us is still on. Deliver the oil and get out of here. Why do you care? She is nothing to you. Why didn't they get the oil from someone else, why you? Get lost, Enzo."

Enzo felt his fists clench and his jaw tighten. "You are a fool," he spat. "Your day will come."

Without a word of reply, Vincenzo placed his hand on the gun. His smile became deadly. Enzo stared at him for a moment and forced himself to turn and walk away, his knuckles whitening as he resisted the urge to leap at Vincenzo and strangle him. *I have to get Laura out of here first,* he thought. But as he departed, he said, "Who would you be without that gun, Vincenzo? Would you be able to stand up to me without it, man to man?"

He stormed out of the house, his mind racing, and jumped into his truck.

⁂

Sarah and Laura eyed the glowing green bath, Sarah smothering giggles and Laura smothering nausea. Sarah turned and sank into a chair in the corner, facing away from Laura, and produced a book from her apron pocket.

Laura looked at the back of Sarah's head and then down at the viscous oil. Despite Sarah's casual slouch, Laura knew the older woman was attuned to her every move. Without removing her clothes, Laura sat cautiously on the lip of the tub and dipped her toe in. She immediately yanked it back, releasing a sharp gasp that caused Sarah to whip around in her chair.

"Cold," Laura said embarrassedly, rubbing her arms and mimicking a shivering.

Sarah smiled amusedly and turned her back again. Laura surveyed the green ooze again, and a scowl of determination came over her face. *Chin up, Laura,* she told herself. *Enzo knows where I am; I just have to buy him and Papa some time.*

Reluctantly, Laura shuffled out of her clothing, shivering, took a deep breath, and submerged her entire foot. The olive oil felt slick, and the cloying smell crowded her nostrils. She smirked despite herself.

I smell like Papa's store, she thought with a chuckle.

She knelt in the bathtub, her knees covered and her arms shiny up to her elbows, gagging and shivering. The tepid oil seemed to leach the warmth from her limbs.

With a belabored sigh, she reclined all the way in the glossy bath. Sarah peeked her head up from her book and, satisfied at Laura's immersion, rose from her chair.

"Let me get you some towels," she said, and exited the room.

Bravely, Laura began to hum "All or Nothing At All." She thought again about her poor father, worried he might get hurt trying to rescue her. She thought about Enzo—her Enzo—and the look in his eyes when he saw her in the kitchen. From that moment, she had known her feelings were real, and the remembrance of that knowledge warmed her heart even as she shivered in the tub.

⟡

Enzo's truck screeched to a stop outside the two-story Milazzo home. Enzo yanked the key out of the ignition, leapt out of the truck, marched to the front door, and let himself in. The house seemed empty, and he hurried through the familiar hallways to the back terrace.

Sophia sat on a reclining chair, her eyes having wandered away from her book and onto the beautiful farmland vista beyond the terrace. As Enzo came flying onto the terrace, she looked up, startled. Her face broke instantly into a huge grin. Enzo's face was pulled into an angry grimace, however, and Sophia's smile faded almost immediately into a look of concern. She rose from her seat, the book falling to the ground, and Enzo pulled her into a hug.

"Sophia," he said, "I need you to help me. I have a plan. I need your help."

"Enzo," she replied, pulling away and studying his face, "what happened?"

"You need to help me," he replied. "Tell me. Does Vincenzo still ask you for dates?"

Sophia's face hardened, her mouth thinning to a line and her jaw clenching in a look of revulsion. She squeezed her eyes shut and swallowed hard before opening them again. "Yes," she replied angrily. "Whenever he sees me. I am repulsed by him."

Enzo looked her in the eye. "Will you trust me to keep you safe?"

Sophia's expression softened. "Of course!"

"Even if I ask you to do something frightening?"

For a moment, Sophia didn't respond, her eyes belying the war going on in her thoughts. "Yes," she said finally, her voice firm as if she were still trying to convince herself. "What's going on?"

"I'll tell you on the way," he replied. "I'm short on time. Will you help me? First I need an extra outfit, some food, and supplies for Laura and myself."

Hesitatingly, Sophia complied with this request, as Enzo seemed quite serious. She quickly went into her home to fetch these items. A few minutes later she returned. "Okay. Let's go. I packed everything I could think of," she said with a sigh.

Enzo's face blossomed into a smile. Sophia flushed a deep scarlet and fought a smile. Enzo kissed the top of her head, missing the sudden look on her face that said she might cry.

Chapter Fourteen

Enzo and Sophia sat in the truck, the dust billowing angrily behind them as he explained everything that had occurred. He tried to cover his plan in detail. He explained what had transpired between himself and Laura on that disastrous night and further explained what happened at Maria and Dominick's house.

"Vito has been crazed trying to find her, and I have been watching Maria's every move," Enzo said. "We knew we were close but had no definite leads, then when Italo appeared, it all became clear. If Italo is around, Vincenzo is not far behind. He asked for ridiculous amounts of oil. He told me where to deliver the oil, and sure enough, Laura was there being held captive and being prepared for a marriage to the Russo's son."

Sophia listened, the shock showing on her face. "Enzo, this is crazy. It sounds like one of your American movies."

He went on to describe how he needed Sophia to be involved, how she would be the decoy to trick Vincenzo and aid Laura out of this nightmare. He gave her explicit details about all the women, the wedding gowns, how many guys were involved, and most important, Vincenzo's gun. He wanted no violence, only a safe and peaceful resolution to this. And for certain he did not want Sophia or Laura hurt.

"Okay, okay, I can do this," she assured him, overcoming her disbelief of the ridiculous situation and plan.

Finally they saw the Russo house looming in the distance. Enzo brought the truck to a halt, and they both took a deep breath and stepped out. Enzo eagerly led the way toward the house, sticking to the shade of the trees that lined the street. Sophia, however, hung back, chewing on her lip for a long while before slowing to a stop.

"Enzo?"

He froze, and turned to look at her over his shoulder. Her face was a canvas of conflicting, tormented emotions. He wanted to comfort her, but did not want to stop, and he felt a stab of guilt mingle with his ever-growing anxiety.

"I'm sorry," he said. "If you're scared, you should go back."

"I am scared."

"That's okay."

"But I'm not scared of them," she said, motioning toward the house and refusing to meet his gaze. "I'm scared for you."

"I shouldn't have brought you with me," he said, looking at the ground. "I'm sorry."

She shook her head and took a deep breath. "Enzo," she said cautiously, looking him in the eye, "maybe you should let her get married."

"But she doesn't want to," he replied, frowning in confusion. "Sophia, I cannot do what you ask. I cannot leave her there. I know she feels the same for me as I do for her, and even if she didn't I couldn't abandon her to this insane plot. I wouldn't let this happen to you."

"How do you know she feels the same?" she asked gently, as if afraid of his response.

He shrugged. "I just know."

"A few nights ago," she said slowly, "she ran away from you. She was trying to get away from you and she did. And maybe . . . maybe you need to let her go."

He looked at her, puzzled. "Why are you saying this?"

"Because . . . I . . ." She shifted uncomfortably from one foot to the other and gave him an exasperated look. "Why don't you let her go?"

"Because I love her," Enzo responded simply.

Sophia looked stunned. "She's a child," she protested.

"It doesn't matter. She is not a child to me"

"It doesn't matter?" she repeated, incredulous.

With a sigh, Enzo turned away from her and started to walk toward the house again. She hurried to keep up with him. "You don't know anything about her!"

He walked on, his shoulders raised defensively.

"You can't even *talk* to her," Sophia said angrily.

He nodded, not really listening.

"You met her, what?" she demanded. "Five or six days ago?"

Pretending not to hear, Enzo stopped and surveyed the house. "Maybe it's best that I go on my own, anyway," he said calmly, hands on his hips. "I know all I need to know."

"I mean, what the hell, Enzo?!" Sophia snapped explosively.

Enzo's patience seemed to evaporate in the same instant. "What is your problem?" he demanded.

"You!" she fired back, the beginnings of tears staining her eyes. "*You* are my problem, you self-obsessed maniac!"

"Who are you to tell me who I can or can't love?" he snapped. "I love Laura."

Sophia jabbed a finger in the direction of the Russo house. "Are you seriously telling me that you can take one look at that American brat and just fall in love with her?"

"Yes, Sophia," he said firmly, "that's what I'm saying! It's more than you think . . . more than you know."

"What about me?" she pleaded, tears streaming down her face.

"What about you?" Enzo asked, confused. "What do my feelings for Laura have to do with you?"

"Are you a complete idiot?" she demanded explosively. "I've been in love with you for years!"

Enzo took a step back as if she'd shoved him, his face a mask of shock and his mouth hanging open. She took a step toward him, her heartbroken look giving way to one of rage. "And you're telling me," she said, sarcasm dripping from her voice, "it takes you only four days to get gooey over some kid who can't even say your name right?"

"I'm telling you," Enzo said quietly, his voice full of hurt, "that doesn't matter to me. It's just a word."

"You're so eager to get off this pathetic island," she snapped, "You'd marry yourself to anyone with an American accent."

"No," he snapped back, scowling. "You are so wrong, Sophia."

She ignored him. "And God forbid," she said, spreading her arms wide and looking up at the sky in a dramatic mimicry of prayer, "you find out if she even likes you or not before you wage war to save her!"

Something in Enzo snapped. "Sophia," he roared, "She does! I know she does! And there's nothing you can do to change that!" He grabbed her by the shoulders and forced her to meet his eye. "I don't want to hurt you. I never would, but if you love me as you say, you need to accept this. I never meant to hurt you. I never would."

"Then don't hurt me," she replied, quietly, looking away from him and away from the house.

Enzo stared at her for a tense moment, wrestling with shame, anger, and confusion. "There is such a thing," he said finally, knowing it would not be sufficient, "as just loving someone without expecting something in return."

"Tell me about it," she muttered.

He studied her face, the face of the best friend he'd ever had, and knew that their friendship had shifted in the last few moments. He wished desperately that he could fix what they'd broken, but he knew there was nothing he could do to remove his feelings for Laura, and no way he could bring himself to feel the way Sophia wanted him to feel.

"And I'm sorry that you don't buy it," he whispered, "but this is real. I love Laura, Sophia. I truly do. I can't change that."

"I don't care, Enzo," she replied, her voice terribly calm. She turned her back to him. "I don't care."

A long, awkward silence followed. Enzo leaned exhaustedly against a tree, staring at her back. "I really am sorry, Sophia. I am. I just—"

"I'm fine," she interjected, turning to face him dry-eyed. After a moment, she spoke again, her voice hesitant. "You could stay here, you know. With me. You could just . . . stay. Maybe . . ."

They looked at each other intensely. "I can't," he said, determinedly holding her gaze. "I . . . can't. I'm sorry. And I can't save her without you. Help me, Sophia. Please, please help me get her out of there."

Enzo looked away, unable to bear the sight of the pain in Sophia's familiar eyes. He gnawed his lip and looked at the house, at his hands, everywhere but at her. She watched him for a moment—silently debating, it seemed—before turning abruptly on her heels and sprinting toward the Russo house.

Confused, it took a moment for Enzo to gather himself and run after her.

❧

Italo sat in the front yard of the Russo house, basking in the shade of a tree. Sophia called out to him and he looked up, rising immediately to his feet. He must have recognized her, because he broke into a broad smile, whistled at her and waved enthusiastically. As Sophia reached him, she consciously straightened her too-big, adrenaline-fueled smile, counting on Italo's slow wits to miss the look of distress she was sure lingered in her eyes.

"I wasn't expecting to see you here today!" Italo said happily.

"Is the American still here?" Sophia asked quickly, wanting to get into the house before Enzo could catch up.

Italo drew himself up proudly and gave her a cocky smile. "I'm driving her to the church myself," he said. "How do you know about her?" he added, but Sophia simply ignored him.

Sophia allowed a mischievous smile to creep over her face. "How long do we have to play a prank on her? I heard she is not too bright; let's mess with her."

His grin broadened, a glimmer of mischief in his eye. He took her hand and led her into the house. Sophia resisted the urge to roll her eyes; Italo was clearly fighting off giggles as they stalked through the halls.

They stopped outside the bathroom door. Italo motioned Sophia to put her ear to the door. She did so, and without warning, he pounded on the door violently. Sophia jumped back, glaring at him, but he was oblivious

"Laura!" he barked authoritatively. "Get out here right now!"

Sophia bit back laughter at the viscous sloshing noise that immediately followed as Laura leapt violently out of the bath. Italo was beside himself with laughter already.

The door flew open and there stood Laura, sheathed in a thin bathrobe that absorbed the oil like bread. She was shiny and slightly green, and her face was red with embarrassment. Her gaze lighted on the laughing Italo, and her eyes sparked with anger. Without hesitation, Laura raised her slimy hand and slapped Italo viciously across the face. Her hand left a streak of green oil behind on his skin.

He lunged for her, but couldn't get a grip on her; his hands slid off when he tried to wrap his fingers around her wrists. Fire in her eyes, Laura smeared as much olive oil on his face as possible, but her feet, still slick, betrayed her. She lost her balance and fell into his arms. Now he laughed again. Glaring daggers at him, she stumbled to regain her footing and squirmed away. The floor was covered with oil, and she gave him a hard shove in the chest that sent him sliding down the hallway. He smacked into a wall and flopped backward on his rear, cursing as he fell.

Satisfied, Laura turned on her heel, marched back into the bathroom, and slammed the door, throwing the lock.

Sophia had used the distraction to slip into the bathroom, and she and Laura stood face to face, sizing each other up.

"What are you doing here, Sophia?" Laura asked finally, exasperated.

"I come . . . to help you," Sophia replied, her broken English reminding her painfully of Enzo's.

"I don't need your help," she snapped haughtily, adjusting the belt of her robe.

Sophia raised an eyebrow. "You . . . want to marry Alfonso?"

"No, I do not!" Laura replied stubbornly, shaking her head. "His hair alone scares me."

"Okay," Sophia replied coolly.

"Okay!"

They faced off for an awkward moment, neither sure what to say or do next.

Sophia finally broke the silence. "You love him?"

Laura looked at her, confused. "Alfonso?"

Sophia shook her head, rolling her eyes. "Enzo."

The directness of the question brought a flustered blush to Laura's cheek. "I don't . . . " She laughed and shook her head, struggling to find the right way to voice her thoughts. "I don't know. What I feel is overwhelming me. Scaring me. I have never felt like this before."

Sophia's face grew cloudy with misunderstanding. "No?"

Laura searched her face, not knowing how to explain herself.

The sound of footsteps in the hallway interrupted their respective thoughts. Laura motioned frantically for Sophia to hide behind a corner cabinet, her eyes shifting frantically between the other girl and the door. Sophia hurried to do as Laura indicated, but the floor was slick and she fought to gain traction, her arms wheeling in the air as she lost her footing. Laura gave her a gentle shove, and Sophia slid across the floor, bumping into the cabinet with a grunt of displeasure.

Sarah's voice snuck in from the other side of the door. "Laura?" She rapped softly on the door before opening it a crack. Sophia just managed to steady herself and disappear behind the cabinet as Sarah entered the room, carrying an armful of coarse-looking towels.

Sarah came to a halt as the door swung shut behind her, her eyes widening as she took a moment to survey the bathroom. Green splatters of oil adorned the walls; more oil had pooled on the floor and splashed across the sink. She looked at Laura in dismayed disbelief. Blushing again, Laura opened her mouth to speak, but she stopped herself.

Sarah stared at Laura for a moment, incredulous. Finally, with a shrug, she gestured for Laura to remove her robe and began vigorously toweling the oil off Laura's skin. She spoke in broken English—an attempt, it seemed, to make Laura feel comfortable.

"Laura," she said as she scrubbed, "Alfonso is a very good boy. A very good son. I give to you my first born . . . with true blessings! I pray one day . . . you love him like I pray for all my children to be loved."

Her words had the opposite effect to what she desired. Laura felt green. Whether it was from the oil or the tragic loving look on Sarah's face, Laura was not sure, but she had no reply.

Enzo slunk through the spacious Russo backyard. The entire space was decked out for a wedding reception, the tables heavily adorned in white flowers and ribbons. The sight made him anxious; the hour of Laura's forced marriage was drawing close. There was no sign of Vito anywhere, and he'd lost sight of Sophia.

Looks like I may have to rescue Laura on my own. I pray Sophia's emotions do not get the best of her. I know her too well. But just maybe she can pull this off, he thought to himself.

A few of Vincenzo thugs patrolled the perimeter of the house, looking bored and sneaking sips of wine and bites of an early dinner. Enzo frequently had to scramble behind trees and under tables to avoid being seen. With every passing minute, his heartbeat quickened.

His mind raced. *I'm running out of time,* he thought frantically. *I'm going to be too late! Sophia failed to go to the bathroom window to indicate that all was in the go mode. I hope she is safe.*

The Russo women bustled around Laura's borrowed bedroom, surrounding Laura and chattering about how beautiful she was and what a wonderful bride she would be. Anxiety made Laura's head swim, and the noise of so many incomprehensible voices only made it worse. The women braided and pinned up her hair, adorning her head with olive flowers. The wedding dress made its dreaded appearance, and they buttoned her in. Laura found herself engulfed in creamy lace and ribbons.

Sarah took her hand and twirled her around. The other women gasped, wiping away tears and cooing affectionately at her, making Laura feel even worse. She caught a glimpse of herself in the sitting room mirror, but she couldn't recognize the woman staring back at her.

One by one, the other women began to filter out of the room, blowing kisses to Laura and patting her hands and cheeks. They all seemed utterly oblivious to her distress. After a few minutes, Laura and Sarah stood alone in the little room. Sarah affixed a wispy veil to Laura's hair, pulling the white lace over Laura's face. Laura shuddered inwardly; the veil felt more like a funeral shroud

Through the veil, Laura saw that Sarah's eyes were teary. Again, a stab of sadness for this lovely woman, who had striven to show her nothing but kindness, pierced Laura's heart. As Sarah began to putter around the room, Laura sank into a chair, struggling with irrational thoughts. She went from telling herself she did not smell like olive oil, to delighting at how soft the bath had made her skin, to thinking of Enzo, and finally to the thought of marrying that short little man called Alfonso.

What if I really did marry him? What if they force me to? What will my life be like then?

Behind the veil, she allowed silent tears to roll once more down her cheeks, riddled with panic and fear. Her thoughts once again brought her to her distressed father. Where was he? Why had he not found her yet? Suddenly she found herself praying, almost as if prayer were something she had just discovered.

❧❧❧

Sophia, who had gone unnoticed in all the commotion, tiptoed out of the bath and through the house. The sound of feminine voices chattering away in other room told her exactly where Laura was.

What am I supposed to do? she thought angrily. *I don't even know where I'm supposed to be looking!*

She passed by an open doorway and came to an astonished halt. *There they are—just as Enzo described.* And then she realized that she had been so immersed in her mission, she'd forgotten to send out the signal to Enzo as he requested. *Oh well,* she thought.

She stepped into the sitting room, surveying the overwhelming mass of white lace and satin and pearls. She allowed her hands to brush the material as she passed, a slow smile of triumph growing on her face. "Hmm, this could be fun," she whispered to herself.

Suddenly, the far-off sounds of women talking to one another grew louder; they were leaving the bedroom. Sophia fled, scurrying down the hallway and out of the house. She took her post on the front terrace beside the door and waited. After a moment, the older women who had helped Laura prepare for the wedding started to file out of the house. They spied Sophia and greeted her affectionately; she responded in kind.

Knowing she needed to hurry, she waved the women over and began hastily and quietly telling them what she knew about the real situation regarding Laura. For various reasons, they had all believed Laura was there willingly. Their giddy smiles gave way to frowns of consternation and exclamations of outrage. At her bidding, they filed around the back of the house.

As the last of them disappeared, Sophia peered one last time toward the front door, just in time to see Sarah and Laura step out onto the terrace. The wind and sun caught the lace of Laura's dress and made it look like sea foam. Sophia could not deny that Laura looked stunning, and she almost hated herself for admitting it.

I promised I'd help you, Enzo, she thought. *She'd better be as lovely on the inside as she looks on the outside, or I'll never forgive you for what I am about to do for you.*

At that moment, two shiny black cars pulled up to the house. Vincenzo and Italo appeared out of nowhere and, after a quick exchange, were handed the keys to the cars by the two other thugs who'd driven the car up. The vehicles were filled with cigarette smoke. Italo whistled at Laura, and Vincenzo rewarded him with an elbow to the ribs. Italo scowled and opened the door of the second car. Sarah slid in immediately, but Laura hesitated. Vincenzo strolled up to her, placing a hand on her shoulder, but she glared at him and shook him off. He waited, his shoulders shaking with mirth, as she eased herself into the car, slamming the door behind her as Italo slid into the driver's seat.

The rest of Vincenzo's gang exited the house and piled into the other car. In a flurry of dust and a thunderous spinning of tires, they took off down the hill. Vincenzo never noticed Sophia.

Suddenly, Enzo's figure appeared from behind a bush on the other side of the house. Sophia watched as he warred with himself, knowing he was thinking of chasing after the cars. After a moment, he seemed to make up his mind, and he disappeared again.

Sophia sent a prayer of good luck after him and turned to go. As she began to venture away from the house, she caught sight of Vito and his little army at the bottom of the hill who by chance were now about to search for Laura in this area. She blanched and ran to meet him quickly. He looked exhausted and emotionally drained.

Sophia filled Vito in briefly, outlining Enzo's rescue plan, feeling a reluctant glow of pleasure as hope rekindled in his eyes. She told him to go to Enzo's truck and Enzo would bring him to the church. Vito felt instant relief, but his anger remained, as his emotions were everywhere.

୧⁙୨

Laura stared somberly out the window, the view of the countryside obscured by her veil. She glanced slyly at Sarah, who sat protectively blocking the locked door. Vincenzo caught her eyes in the rearview mirror and winked. She was beginning to grow frantic; her mind raced. She was not going to marry this stranger; they couldn't make her. But "what if?" kept resonating in her head. She felt claustrophobic, and she knew Vincenzo was reading her mind.

What if they threaten my papa?

What if they hurt Enzo?
What if they use the gun to make me say yes?
What if? What if? What if?

The cars eased to a stop next to a small church. Loud organ music reached the car, and an enormous white ribbon hung over the door, making the whole building look like an undesirable present. A buzzing throng of guests stood on the lawn, chatting excitedly. At the sight of the car, they burst into applause and started to file eagerly into the church.

The men filed out of the cars. Italo paced eagerly to the side of the car and opened the door for Sarah and Laura. Sarah hopped out immediately, but Laura hung back. With an exasperated huff, Vincenzo slid out of the car, slamming the door behind him, and stalked to the door, reaching out his hand and leveling a terrifying glare at Laura.

Laura reluctantly took the outstretched hand and stepped out of the car. She wanted to flee, but her mind kept conjuring images of guns. Vincenzo escorted Laura to the door of the church as the last of the crowd disappeared inside. Don Russo, Alfonso's father, and Sarah stood waiting at the door. They beamed at Laura. Italo pulled open the door of the church for them and ushered Laura and the others into the cool dimness of the vestibule.

Maria rushed into the vestibule to meet them, immediately taking ownership of Laura's free hand and playing the role of her mother. "Didn't I tell you I would make it all right this time?" she said to Laura. "Just wait until you see that handsome boy at the altar waiting for you."

Maria smothered Laura in a crushing hug, and Laura stiffened at her touch and her smell. Laura decided she would rather smell like olive oil than smell the way Maria did.

The inner vestibule doors swung open and shut as Don Russo and Sarah entered the sanctuary, and Laura tensed. Her eyes darted wildly for an escape. Enzo was nowhere to be seen, and Sophia, it seemed, had abandoned her. She had no idea where Vito was. Vincenzo, Italo, and the rest of the thugs sensed her desire to flee, and they crowded closer to her; there was no way out.

Some help you were, Sophia, she thought, suddenly and bitterly. *You didn't even* try *to do anything!*

The music inside the church suddenly changed, and all the men looked at her expectantly. Italo pulled the inner door open again, but Laura didn't move. Vincenzo came up behind her, pulling his jacket open and flashing his gun. He looked her dead in the eye.

"Alfonso told me he would rather have a dead bride than a runaway bride," he said.

Laura's imagination ran through a variety of escape scenarios:

Laura kneed Vincenzo in the chest. Italo tackled her. Gunshot.

Laura slipped out of his grasp. She bolted for the car. Gunshot.

Laura scrambled up to the roof. She slipped. Gunshot.

Laura paled, shuddered, and shook Vincenzo off her. With squared shoulders, she marched through the doors and into the aisle of the sanctuary.

Chapter Fifteen

*L*aura stood in the doorway as her eyes adjusted to the darkness. Vincenzo and Italo slipped into the church and swung the doors shut behind her. The church was packed with people who stood when Laura entered. A quartet played boisterously. Laura wavered at the door and fought the urge to turn around and flee. The echoes of her imagined gunshots still rang in her head.

Enzo reached the church in record time, having taken a bumpy farm road at a frightening speed and praying the whole way that his truck wouldn't stall. Vito and Enzo had minimal exchange during the drive. Both were distraught and on a mission, waging the war in their own minds and in their own way.

Enzo had parked the truck in an inconspicuous place not far down the road from the church and taken the remainder of the distance on foot. Vito was grateful to be this close to his daughter, but there was no sight of Laura when he arrived, dusty and out of breath, and for a moment, he panicked. The sight of the crowd outside calmed his nerves, however; they would all have been inside the church if Laura had already arrived.

Good, he thought. *I made it in time.*

Enzo allowed himself to become engulfed in the crowd, figuring it would help him blend in, but regretted it almost immediately when he couldn't extricate himself again. He tried to free himself, but couldn't disentangle himself from the crowd, and he watched helplessly as the two black cars pulled up in front of the church. Enzo only saw her as a mass of white lace, half-hidden by eagerly applauding wedding guests, before he was sucked into the church. Laura had not noticed him, and he tried to remain invisible.

He sat among the other wedding guests, listening to the organist battering away at the creaky-voiced old instrument for what seemed like hours. He watched Don Russo enter with his wife, and saw them grinning proudly at Alfonso, who stood waiting at the altar.

Then the music changed, the doors opened, and Laura glided in, heavily surrounded by an array of characters.

From the far wall of the church, Enzo watched her, his breath lodged in his throat at the look on her face. He was like a compressed spring, taut with energy, and he struggled to suppress the urge to scream or cry.

⚘

Laura took a big breath in and a tiny, reluctant step forward. Her eyes scanned the church.

Alfonso stood at the altar, looking surprisingly handsome. He stared eagerly at her, a giant smile stretched across his face. For the first time, the full realization of how short he was entered Laura's mind. She looked at his feet; he was standing on a sizeable soda crate to make himself look taller, and still Laura knew she would tower over him.

"This can't be," she said aloud. "I don't know him, and I do not want to marry him."

Vincenzo was the only one to hear her. He grabbed the skin of her upper arm and twisted it. Laura let out a squeal of pain, and stubbornly suppressed tears finally emerged.

"Keep walking, princess," he snarled in her ear. "Tonight you will be squealing like a pig. You won't remember anything after tonight!"

Laura wanted to vomit. She wept despite herself and tried to imagine herself with Alfonso. It all felt so wrong to her. She longed for her father and wondered where on earth he could be.

Again, Laura's imagination ran through various scenarios. She saw herself as an older woman and holding the hand of a small child, eating dinner with her family, laughing and smiling, and getting into a warm bed each night. In each imagined scene, there was a man's torso, but no face.

Her eyes swept the guests, and her mouth fell open as she made eye contact with Enzo. Everything but his face dissolved out of her vision, and she stood riveted in place, relieved beyond words to know he was there.

Enzo smiled sadly and motioned to Vincenzo, who failed to notice the exchange. The gesture spoke of danger. Laura wrestled her gaze away from Enzo and continued down the aisle, knowing the uproar that would ensue if Vincenzo saw him.

Laura's reluctant steps brought her finally to the altar. She looked down through the veil at the beaming Alfonso. Slowly, he reached up, lifted the veil away from her face, and took her hands.

No! her mind screamed. *This can't be!*

Suddenly, the doors to the church swung open. A figure in white —no, a white wedding dress!—stood framed by the doorway and bathed in sunlight. A veil obscured the woman's face, but Laura knew instantly that it was Sophia. Another bride. The crowd was frozen.

Color began to return to Laura's ashen face as Sophia began to run down the aisle toward her. The music ground to a cacophonous halt, but no one moved; every face in the room but Enzo's had become a picture of shock. The unsuspecting guests watched, stunned, as Sophia reached the altar.

"We look the same," Laura said in an awestruck whisper. "Please tell me what to do."

Sophia smiled and took her hand. They stared at each other for a moment, beaming and radiant, before they turned back to face the crowd. As if in slow motion, they ran back up the aisle, the white gowns billowing out behind them like sails.

As they ran toward the door, a crowd of women in wedding dresses came pouring into the church. They flooded the aisle, and Sophia and Laura vanished among them. These were the older women who had helped dress Laura, the younger girls who had taught her how to cook, and the grim-faced women who had joined Vito's search all over the countryside that day. They had all gathered to rescue Laura. They spread and ran all around the church, forming a barrier around Sophia and Laura and blocking Vincenzo, Italo ,and the other gangsters from getting anywhere near them.

For a moment, the crowd was silent. Dominick and Maria watched from the pews, their faces ashen. Suddenly, Maria rose, her face a wild mask of horrific rage, and her shrieks rang out through the church. "No!" she screamed. "This can't happen! No! Someone stop her, grab her! She must marry Alfonso!"

The congregation dissolved into hysteria. Alfonso's family struggled to stop the crowd of white-gowned rescuers; Alfonso himself fell backward off his soda crate. Over the milling crowd, Maria's piercing wails of rage reached the yard outside. It was a loud chaos inside the church. Laura choked back tears as she clutched Sophia's hand and ran.

They barreled out the doors, dashing headlong across the yard. The sudden peace of the countryside and the sight of the setting sun nearly brought Laura to her knees, but she kept up with Sophia, unwilling to risk her newfound freedom. As they ran, Laura saw her father—her dear papa—rushing toward her. His expression of indescribable joy made her heart soar, but he stopped only long enough to clutch her hand for a brief moment.

"Laura, run!" he shouted over his shoulder, carrying on in the direction of the church. "I will find you! Tomorrow we leave this God-forsaken place! Now run!"

The doors flew open again as he reached the steps, and Laura lost sight of him among the stream of white dresses that issued forth from the building. The women scattered in all directions, running as fast as their feet would carry them. Vincenzo's confused thugs gave chase, dashing across the open fields in scattered chaos.

Vito thundered into the church, his face red with rage, and stormed through the still-frantic crowd, hunting for Maria. As soon as he laid eyes on her, standing enveloped in Dominick's arms, his anger came to a head, and he bulled his way across the church to confront her. All the panic that covered Maria's face gave way to fear as he approached, and her knuckles went white as she clutched at the front of Dominick's shirt.

"Vito, what is happening?" Dominick pleaded. "Laura was just here, and—"

Vito held up a hand, and Dominick's begging died in his throat. Thirty years of pent-up anger and buried secrets boiled forth from Vito's lips.

"Dominick," he said, "it's time you knew the truth! The baby that you thought was yours—the one Maria claimed to have adopted—was my daughter, Ana, your niece. Maria had her kidnapped and sent to you telling you some tale that her birthmother died in childbirth. I was foolish enough to believe she meant well when she came to help me. I, too, believed you had a good woman. She never told you the hell she put me through. She never answered my letters. I had to pay to get my own daughter back to me. I had to have my own baby kidnapped. She made it impossible for me to come here, or for Ana to be returned legally if I had."

Dominick's startled eyes shifted from his brother to his wife and back again. Vito swallowed a stab of guilt and pressed on.

"It took me months to get Ana back. Maria told you that your baby had died. But that baby you still mourn is my child. Another lie; my Ana is alive and well and happily married. I took back what was rightfully mine, and I refuse to let this woman—" he jabbed a finger at Maria like a knife "—harm my family ever again. She is insane. She was then and still is now. That baby you mourned all those years was mine. How insane is this?

"Maria is the reason we haven't spoken in thirty years," Vito continued, swallowing a sob. "She is a vile, small-minded witch." He looked away from Dominick's stricken face and turned a murderous glare on Maria. "As God is my witness, Maria, you will rot in hell. God, help me from killing her. I confess here in front of God how the thought of that has given me pleasure for the last thirty years."

Vito spat at her feet. Dominick stared at him, horrified and paralyzed by his brother's anguish. Vito wanted nothing more than to break Maria's neck with his bare hands, but he forced himself to turn away. As he shoved his way through the now-silent crowd, that hated voice rose up behind him.

"You were and still are a worthless man!" Maria shouted after him, a note of smug triumph in her voice. "That baby never belonged in your care! That baby needed me, not you, a mother. You never deserved children!"

All sense now fled from Vito's mind. He turned and strode back toward Maria, blind with rage. Maria, finally realizing she may have gone too far, looked to Dominick with desperation in her eyes. "Dominick," she cried, "save me, help me! Your brother is crazy!"

Too late. Vito's hand closed around the ugly woman's neck, reducing her cries to gasps.

Dominick was speechless, struggling to piece all of the events together. The supposed death of Ana—or, as he knew her, the little girl that they had lost to asphyxiation—had devastated him. Baby Alessandra was the name they had given her. He had mourned her for many years and still carried her photo in his wallet. His heart broke again, and he began to cry like a baby.

Maria clutched desperately at the hand around her neck, trying to free herself, but Vito did not loosen his grip. "Let me make myself perfectly clear," he said in a level, deadly voice. "This is the last time you will interfere with my family. You will never get close enough to my children ever again to even think of harming them. Thank God my son has been spared from you.

"I am going to kill you. How dare you meddle with my family? How dare you try to dictate my daughter's fate? How dare you kidnap her? What God has not given you, you feel you have the right to take and control from others, mainly me. God can judge me as he pleases, but I refuse to allow you to get away with this a second time. You deserve to die, you ugly barren bitch, and I am going to be the one to see it happen! But before you go, you will admit to Dominick all the evil you have done to me, to my children, and to my poor brother. Tell him the truth, now!"

Maria spat on Vito and tried to squirm away, realizing with horror that Vito was in earnest; he fully intended to kill her. Vito's grip tightened on her throat. Maria was red in the face and gasping for air.

"You have no heart," he snarled. "No one with decency would do this to another person, and certainly not to two innocent children. I had to pay to get my own daughter back. Admit it, you worthless *boutana*! Tell my brother the truth, now!"

Maria's eyes were bloodshot, and she looked at Dominick pleadingly.

"Tell him the truth!" Vito roared.

He slackened his grip enough for Maria to draw a breath. Somehow, this sudden release terrified Maria more than his stranglehold had, and suddenly the whole story came flooding out of her mouth. Alfonso's family had searched high and low to find someone for him to marry. No one ever dared to speak openly of the disgrace of Alfonso's height or the fact that no girl would agree to marry him. When Maria had learned that Vito and Laura were coming from America, she developed a plan—one that would serve the purpose of revenging herself upon Vito on top of the huge monetary reward offered by the Russo family in exchange for her services.

She had not shared her plan with Dominick, of course. Dominick was a kind and simple man. He could never intuitively sense ill will in others, and he took everything at face value. This aspect of his nature had served Maria well over the years. Vito had destroyed her plans again, and as she spluttered the last of her story out and Vito's grip tightened again on her neck, she screamed.

Dominick finally intervened, crying, "Let her go! Please, Vito! I love her! I am sorry; I never knew!"

The crowd gawked, terrified by the scene. No one dared approach Vito. Vito refused to hear Dominick's pleading now. "You used my brother's goodness as a weakness for all these years," he spat at Maria, "and now you will pay."

Complete silence rang in the church then. It was tense and cold. Dominick was too horrified to speak again, and Maria was still struggling. Suddenly, something came flying through the air and met the back of Vito's head. Stunned, he dropped to his knees, his hand falling limply from Maria's neck. Maria staggered into Dominick's open arms. Vito was not bleeding, but he was stunned. Suddenly he saw the rock that hit him as he looked around. A lump quickly began to grow where he had been hit.

"Why?" was all, Dominick could say. "Why, my love?"

Vito made a fruitless attempt to stand. Suddenly a shot rang out. Chaos ensued. People dropped to the ground in fear, first in silence, then in hysteria. No one saw who had pulled the trigger.

Maria, the recipient of the bullet, fell backward, blood sputtering from her shoulder. It did not appear to be a fatal wound, but she howled as if it were, her voice hoarse and cracking. Some people flocked to her side, others to Vito's. Dominick stood stock-still, too shocked to move either way. "Maria, my Maria!" was all that came out of his mouth.

Vito's threat was forgotten. Slowly, whispers gave way to open argument as the guests tried to sort out who the gunman was once they realized he had departed from the church. Vito took the opportunity to disappear into the crowd as the paramedics arrived. One last look back at his brother's stricken face nearly broke his will, so he turned his back and strode away as quickly as he could. He was disgusted with himself at this point. His lack of self-control frightened him.

Peter and Giovanni stood waiting for him at the back of the church. They had helped Enzo clear a path for his getaway and had come looking for Vito. The scene they witnessed was far worse than anything they had expected to ensue, and they were relieved to see Vito was unharmed.

"I gave you as long as I could to make your point," Peter told Vito, waving at him with his trusty slingshot. "But then I had to knock some sense into you, to stop you from wasting your life. Maria is not worth much; it would have done you no good to kill her. It wouldn't have undone the past."

Vito gave the aged man a nod of approval. He knew what had just transpired bordered on insanity. But thirty years of holding in his rage over what had happened, and now, to have it happen again was more than he could bear. He thought forgiveness might one day be possible, but he realized this wound was way too deep. He was tormented for his brother and felt remorse for his poor behavior inside a church. It revealed the worst of him and perhaps his own evil. He was not familiar with this at all.

The men stepped out of the way as the crowd parted and the paramedics rushed out of the church, toting the moaning yet listless Maria on a stretcher. Dominick came hurrying in her wake, throwing Vito a sincerely apologetic glance as he passed. The guests began to file out of the church. Vito took a few moments to gather his wits and made his way back to the altar, pushing against the flow of the crowd, to reach Alfonso's side. The young man was sitting on his crate with his head in his hands.

"Go find real love, son," Vito said kindly, bending down to pat Alfonso's shoulder. "You will find it one day. Cry no tears. This was never meant to be."

Alfonso heaved a sigh and raised his eyes to meet Vito's. "I am sorry for all of this and all of us," he said. Then he rose to his feet, a look of grim determination on his face and a glimmer of hope in his eye, and held out his hand for a sincere handshake.

Vito replied, "I am sorry as well for my poor behavior."

Sophia and Laura ran through a field together, long grasses whipping at their ankles. Vincenzo tore after them. They rounded a bend, and there was a breathless Enzo and his truck. His eyes widened in horror at the sight of Vincenzo thundering in their wake. As soon as his eyes met Laura's, they both released a strangled cry. Laura ran straight to him, and he swung her up into his arms.

Sophia, looking crestfallen, slowed to a stop as she reached Enzo's side and spun to face Vincenzo. Vincenzo skidded to a halt a few feet away, red-faced and scowling. The four stood in a moment of suspension. No one seemed ready to speak. Sophia glared at Vincenzo; Vincenzo scowled at Enzo, who scowled back; and Laura looked up at Enzo's face as if silently willing him to just get into the truck and drive away.

Vincenzo regained composure first. He looked at Laura, then Enzo, as if trying to decide who angered him more, and puffed up his chest, squaring his shoulders. He reached into the pocket of his now-sweat-soaked jacket and pulled his gun out of his pocket. He took a step toward Enzo and Laura and raised the weapon.

Enzo's eyes went wide, and he immediately stepped in front of Laura, barring Vincenzo from coming within reach of her. The gesture startled Laura and Sophia, and seemed to throw Vincenzo off balance. The men faced off.

"Give her to me," Vincenzo ordered harshly, his breath still coming in exhausted gasps.

Enzo responded, "Or what?"

Vincenzo's scowl deepened, and he cocked the hammer of the gun. Immediately, Sophia stepped between him and Enzo, her eyes level with the barrel, and stared Vincenzo in the eye.

"You will have to shoot me, too, Vincenzo."

Vincenzo seemed to instantly deflate then. His shoulders dropped and his scowl disappeared, and he let out a heavy sigh. The gun went limp in his hand.

"Ah, I'm tired of this, Enzo," he said, his voice tinged with regret. He looked at Laura and said, "Is this the guy you spoke of?"

Laura's heart was pounding heavily, and she simply nodded.

He looked at Enzo now and said, "I see how you feel about this girl. I didn't know she came here for you. I always thought . . . I always thought it was you and Sophia . . ." His voice trailed away, and he sighed again. A half-smile flashed across his face.

Laura perked up and said, "Vincenzo, is this the girl you spoke of? With Enzo taken, maybe now Sophia will finally see you."

Sophia cringed ever so slightly. Vincenzo saw, and his face fell again. He stared at the ground for a moment. Suddenly, his head snapped up, and he threw a look over his shoulder as if just remembering he was not the only one who was after Laura.

"Go, get out of here," he urged, meeting Enzo's eye again. "Quick, before the others catch up!"

Enzo's eyebrows shot up. "Really, Vincenzo?" he asked, unable to hide the awe in his voice. "I never expected this from you. You steal from others—good, kind, hardworking people. You've acted like a coward so many times. Kidnapping and holding girls against their will is an all-time low. Your poor mother cries for you all the time, and she does not deserve to weep for you." A note of compassion entered his voice. "You could be so much more than a thug. Make something of yourself, Vincenzo; I know you can. Sophia is a good girl. She will never see you if you do not change. There is still time to make something better of yourself."

Vincenzo's jaw clenched for a moment, and his fingers tightened around the gun again. A look of uncertainty flashed in his eyes, as if he regretted giving Enzo the chance to speak at all. He locked eyes with Enzo over Sophia's shoulder, but there was nothing he could do. He was butter in Sophia's presence. Finally, he lowered the gun to his side and looked away, breaking eye contact with Enzo.

Sophia stepped forward and took the gun from Vincenzo's hand, careful not to touch him as she did so. Vincenzo's mouth fell open in surprise, but she scowled at him and turned away, clutching the gun in her hand, and marched away to stand beside the truck, staring down at the road.

Enzo opened the truck door and helped Laura into the passenger seat. Then he turned back to Vincenzo and extended his hand.

Vincenzo accepted it, and they shook. Vincenzo seemed to gain strength from this exchange; he stood taller, straighter, and prouder.

Enzo turned and made his way back to the truck and touched Sophia on the shoulder. She turned to him and placed her hands on his cheeks, searching his eyes desperately, but she knew that what she was looking for wasn't there. She dropped her hands and kissed him on the cheek before reluctantly stepping away. She looked up at Laura for a moment, then walked slowly to the side of the truck and embraced her with her free arm.

"You are one lucky girl," she said. "They don't make men better than Enzo. Cherish him."

She turned and walked purposefully away, Vincenzo's gun held out from her body like a dirty towel. Enzo watched her go, a figure in white marching alone down the dirt road, before he scrambled into the truck. Vincenzo was the only one left to watch as the truck sped off in the opposite direction, kicking up dust as it screeched away.

Chapter Sixteen

*E*nzo and Laura drove through the countryside with the windows down. Wind whipped through Laura's hair and sent the bridal veil flapping wildly all over the cabin of the truck. Enzo's white-knuckled hands gripped the steering wheel, and his mouth had become a grim line.

"Tomorrow morning, early . . . you must get on the train to Rome," he told her. "Your father has tickets," he continued. "I will keep you safe tonight and then tomorrow you go. Okay? Please give me tonight, just so we can talk. That's all I ask. I can't let you go without taking that chance to get to know you."

Laura just stared at him, her expression unreadable. Enzo stared out through the windshield. A moment of windy silence passed between them, while Enzo struggled not to turn and look at her, afraid of what he might see in her eyes. After a moment, he snuck a peek. Instant smiles came over their faces when their eyes met. Laura threw her head back and laughed.

"Thank you, Enzo!" she crowed, pulling the veil out of her hair and tossing it onto the floor.

Laura had come out of her kidnapping with an expanded awareness of the opportunities life offered. She had to be alone with Enzo; she needed to be reassured of his love. She wanted more of Italy, this culture, but mostly she wanted more of him. She wanted to teach him about America. She wanted to teach him to speak English like an American. She wanted to speak to him in his native language and tell him how she felt.

She was ready to let go completely and trust that Teresa had known what she was doing when she had orchestrated their love. Perhaps Teresa really was up there, smiling and dancing. With that, Laura let go of any concerns she had for her father. She would meet him at the station in the morning, but for now, Enzo was her sole focus.

The truck stopped behind the small movie theater. Enzo and Laura raced out of the truck and into the lobby of the building, locking the doors behind them. Laura exhaled deeply at the final bolt sounded.

The ornate lobby's richly decorated walls, thick carpeting, and elegant chandeliers nearly took her breath away. It seemed to belong to a different part of the world. She walked slowly through the space, marveling at its grandeur, and into the theater. She walked down the center aisle, running her fingers along the backs of the red velvet chairs. There was a reverent silence here, a careful elegance that starkly contrasted with the ruggedness of the town outside.

She stood in the middle of the theater. Golden light bulbs glowed softly and cast halos of warm light around her, illuminating the sensual curves of a heavy velvet curtain that hung sleepily over the screen. The bulbs dimmed suddenly as the red curtain sighed slowly open. Laura gasped and turned as the projector clicked on. Light streamed out from the elevated window of the projection booth.

Laura found herself bathed in light as the first scenes of *Sherlock, Jr.* flickered across the screen. She stood in the aisle and watched the movie begin, enthralled. After a few moments, a hand tapped her shoulder and she turned. Enzo stood silhouetted by the streaming light. He extended his hand to her and she took it. Chills ran up her spine at his touch.

They exited the theater and reentered the lobby. Enzo opened a small door behind the ticket counter and disappeared into the darkness beyond. Laura smiled and followed, the murmurs of the first lines of dialogue in the film echoing faintly behind her.

Laura followed Enzo up a small spiral staircase, the music from the movie muffled as the door swung shut behind her. She fumbled for Enzo's hand in the dim light. He led her upward until they reached a small landing. It was dusty and grimy, nothing like the exuberant, gilded décor of the theater. Enzo paused in front of another small door and motioned for Laura to open it. Smiling and curious, she pushed the door open and entered the projection booth.

It was a small space, crammed with rickety equipment and boxes of movie reels. The projector ticked loudly. Enzo had placed tiny mirrors in the corners of the projection booth to catch the light from the projector. They splashed pools of light into the booth, a warm, ever-shifting glow that trembled like light filtering through tree branches.

Laura smiled and shook her head in amazement. Enzo watched her closely, barely breathing. The movie rolled heedlessly on in front of them, its noise muffled in the space. Laura sank into a stool on one side of the projector, and Enzo sat on a stool on the other. They watched the movie in silence for a few minutes.

"Enzo?"

"Yes, Laura?"

"Will you help me with this dress?"

She fluffed the poufy mass of white skirts at him, and he smiled a bashful smile.

It was a two-person job, a convoluted mass of snaps, buttons, and buckles among seemingly endless satin and lace. Laura had been sewn into the gown, and Enzo had to gnaw at the stitching to release her. The dress came away in a flutter of ruffles and lace and pooled on the floor, leaving Laura in a simple smock.

Enzo touched her hand softly and helped her out of the costume. They were both red in the face, and Laura busied herself with folding the dress to avoid meeting his eye. Her body reacted to his touch and her own state of half-undress in ways she had never experienced before.

"Laura?"

Laura looked up at him expectantly, her cheeks burning. "Yes, Enzo?"

Her eyes were wide and he fumbled for the right words. "May I kiss you?"

She nodded. He looked relieved and slowly placed his lips on hers.

What they lacked in verbal communication skills, they made up for with passion. One kiss gave way to another, and another. They leaned against the wall and fell to the floor in a heap, arms encircling each other. When Laura was finally able to pull back and look into his eyes, she saw the answers. She knew what she felt was undeniable. All the answers she needed were in his eyes, his touch, and his kisses. They held each other tightly for what seemed forever. It felt safe. It felt right.

After what seemed to be far too short a time, Enzo left the booth. Alone, Laura looked around the space. A stack of papers resting on a shelf caught her eye, and she pulled out a thick stack of letters. She turned them over and recognized her own handwriting.

She smiled, looking up as Enzo reentered the room. He was holding a small basket of bread, fruit and cheese, and he grinned when he saw her holding the letters.

"You kept them," Laura said.

He shrugged and started to unpack the basket. "Of course."

She flipped through them and found the first one she sent him. She scanned it, chuckled at her writing. "It's crazy. When I wrote this, I had no idea . . . "

"No idea?" he questioned.

She looked at him seriously for a moment, before she blushed and dropped her gaze. She looked back at the letters. He smiled to himself as he assembled sandwiches.

"Why did you write to me?" she asked.

Smiling, he answered, "Teresa asked me to."

A moment of silence fell between them. "I miss her," Laura admitted.

"I wonder how she knew . . ." Enzo said, his voice trailing off as Laura smiled at him.

"Knew what?" she asked.

He met her eye, but averted his gaze almost instantly. "I made you a sandwich," Enzo said quickly, changing the subject.

He motioned to the ground, and Laura noticed that he had laid out a thin blanket with pillows for seats. She smiled and sank to the floor. They ate in silence. Occasionally, they made eye contact and smiled before averting their eyes again.

"Enzo, I . . ." Laura began. He looked at her expectantly, and she lost courage. "I love this sandwich," she said at last.

He smiled and nodded. "I am very good at making sandwiches," he replied playfully.

"Will you show me the rest of the theater?" she requested.

Enzo nodded eagerly. She got up and offered Enzo her hand to help him stand. He stood, keeping his fingers intertwined with hers. They exited the booth and hurried, giggling, down the stairs.

Laura took off as soon as they reached the lobby, dashing into the theater and scampering down the aisle. Enzo followed. She ran down a row of seats, rounded the end, and then dashed back to the aisle and into another row. Enzo had to leap over the backs of the chairs to keep up with her.

She doubled over in laughter when he almost caught her. She evaded him and ran to the front of the theater, pressing her back against the screen.

He caught up to her and, with a sly look on his face, opened an unseen door that stood in the shadows of the open curtain. She gave him a gleefully grin and disappeared inside.

They wandered around in the bleak, cavernous space behind the movie screen, their feet leaving eerie footprints in the dust. Enzo turned on a few of the backstage lights and maneuvered them so that Laura's shadow stretched across the screen and washed away Buster Keaton's face. She smiled at her shadow and danced about, mimicking Buster Keaton's antics, her shadow jumping across the screen. They acted out the last scene of the movie, their shadows falling almost perfectly over the actors on the screen. Laura gasped with laughter as Enzo kissed her hands, but managed to slide out of his grasp before the final kiss.

She scampered back out of the theater and into the booth as Enzo turned off the lights and hurried after her. They sat in the projection booth for hours, a growing mess of film reels springing up around them as they whiled away the time. Enzo showed Laura a scene from *The Bicycle Thief,* and they both had tears of sadness on their cheeks while savoring the last of the food, feeding each other, sipping from one glass, and falling deeply in love.

The hour had grown very late. They were exhausted. Laura yawned, rubbed her eyes, and looked at Enzo, smiling sadly. He tossed her a pillow and she lay down on top of the blanket, shivering. Enzo rummaged around and produced yet another, somewhat dustier blanket, looking at Laura apologetically before covering her shoulders with it. Then he lay down a few feet away, and she frowned, offering him the blanket instead.

"Oh, no. I don't get cold," he said. "Besides, when I went to get Sophia today, she packed some supplies for me and a change of clothes for you. She was very helpful."

Laura smirked at him. They lay on the floor, looking at each other for a long time and fighting sleep. They did not want to waste their time together, but their mutual exhaustion finally overtook them, and they drifted off. An hour or so later, Laura lay on her back, blinking away sleep and a million emotions.

"Enzo?" she called softly, turning to look at him, the dim light making him little more than a shadow. "Enzo, are you asleep?"

"Yes," he mumbled into his pillow.

"Enzo," she said quietly. "Can I . . ? I want to talk to you."

With his eyes still closed, Enzo turned to face her. "Okay. Laura, lets talk." But first he had to stop kissing every inch of her face.

"Are you too tired?"

"No."

"Me, neither."

"Okay."

There was a very long pause. Blinking his eyes sleepily, Enzo asked, "Laura?"

"Enzo, I think . . ." she began. Her voice faltered. "I want to tell you something."

He sat up, looking at her expectantly. She sat up as well, took a deep breath, and swallowed hard. "Enzo Fellini, "I think I lo—"

"Stop," he said. "Don't say that." He turned his back to her and flopped down, his shoulders hunched protectively.

Laura blinked, stunned. "What?"

"I don't want to hear that," Enzo said sadly.

Laura sat up straighter. "What? Enzo? But I thought . . . "

He turned around to face her again. "Three or four nights ago, you ran from me. Remember?"

"Enzo, I—"

"You say we can't talk."

"That was different," she insisted. "I was crazy, my body was hurting, and my brain was playing tricks on me. You have a sister; you have to understand."

Enzo was surprised he hadn't thought of that before. "Ah, okay, okay," he said. He could see how uncomfortable she was with this topic, but happy that she had shared with him. Then he explained his reasoning. "You leave tomorrow," he said, sitting up with a pained expression on his face. "Forever!"

"Enzo . . . "

"And then I may never see you again," he whispered.

"Enzo, I'm sorry!" she cried, realizing she wasn't ready to go back to New York, not without him. "I know I'm asking too much of you, but I can't go back to New York without telling you how I feel."

"No, Laura."

"You don't get to say no!"

"No, no, no!" Enzo insisted, looking away with tears in his eyes.

Near tears herself, Laura cried, "I thought you felt the same way!"

"Goddamn it, Laura!" he exclaimed, turning to look pleadingly at her again. "Of course I do! I fought for you, Laura. I broke Sophia's heart for you. I have known from the moment Teresa told me about you . . . I just knew. I love you like nothing I have ever loved. You changed me, Laura. I want you to stay. I want to spend my life with you. I will take care of you, always, and I will work to give you an amazing life. I will be loyal to you, *per sempre*. Please give us a chance? If you go it will be impossible, do you see this?

A stunned silence fell. Suddenly, Laura remembered something, and, fumbling around in the dimness, she found her shoe. From it, she pulled the penny she had found at the Russo house. She handed it to him. "I found this yesterday. It's from the year you were born. I knew you would come for me. I just knew it."

Enzo was so familiar with pennies that, even in the half-darkness, he knew exactly what it was. He swallowed hard. He deliberated with himself for a moment, then rose to his feet, reaching up and grasping a small box that sat hidden on a high shelf in the booth. He hesitated for a moment, then gingerly handed her the box. She tried the lid and, after a few seconds of tugging, it sprung open.

Dozens of American pennies cascade out of the box, covering her lap and the floor around her in copper. The sea of coins caught what little light there was and threw it up into their faces. She stared in unabashed awe at the pennies, picking them up one after the other to study the dates until she became completely overwhelmed. Each one had the same year: 1932—the year Laura was born. Laura laughed in amazement.

She looked down at the box again, and noticed a folded piece of paper tucked into the bottom of it. She pulled it out gingerly and looked at Enzo. He smiled and nodded, and she unfolded it. It was a letter addressed to her, written in Enzo's careful handwriting. She handed it to him.

"Will you read this to me?" she asked.

Enzo's eyes darted across the page. He frowned and shook his head saying, "I wrote this before . . . before I knew you. Before I *really* knew you."

He inhaled deeply and read, shakily. "I look at you, and in your eyes I see the sky at dawn. I see the sky when it's full of stars. I see the sky when it's impossibly blue. I look into your eyes and I see your laughter as a child. I see your determination and the careful way you interact with people. I look at you and I imagine you as an old woman. I see the way you imagine me as an old man. I look at you and I know, already, that I've given you my future. That no matter what happens, I'm going to live the rest of my life for you. I knew that when I met you, and I know it now."

For a long moment, he stared at the paper, afraid to meet her eyes. Finally, he looked at her, and her face was glowing. She didn't break her gaze from his face. He felt suddenly shy.

"Not in English enough?" he asked.

"No, Enzo. It was perfect," she said. She leaned forward over the pool of pennies, and they moved with her in jingling waves of copper.

They looked at each other intensely for a moment, and then Laura moved forward again and kissed him. He laughed as she kissed him, and she leaned into him further. She laughed, too. Their breath came in short, happy bursts. They both knew letting go was not an option any longer.

The next morning found them sleeping close together, their arms and legs intertwined. Enzo was respectful and never even attempted to push for more. Embracing and kissing Laura after this last week was all he could have hoped for. This morning, he stirred first. He consulted a small pocket watch and jolted awake, his eyes wide. He leaned over Laura to wake her and froze, watching her sleep for a moment, his heart warmed with love. He stroked her cheek and smiled sadly as her lashes fluttered. He kissed her gently, and her eyes opened. She smiled at him, sleep still heavy in her eyes.

"Time to go," he announced quietly.

She yawned, stretched, looked at him sadly, and kissed him for a long time. Finally she had to get up and make herself presentable once again for her father. She was thankful to Sophia for the clothing that she provided, although it was a bit big. She taunted Enzo, saying, "Well now is your chance if you want Sophia." They both laughed.

It was early dawn. The sun was barely up. Yellow, buttery light illuminated Vito as he stood on the platform with his and Laura's luggage. He was shaking with exhaustion, and his eyes were bloodshot. He checked his watch compulsively as the minutes ticked by, suspicion and fear ever growing in his mind.

Enzo's truck pulled up next to the station just as the train appeared on the horizon. Laura and Enzo clambered out of the truck, clasping each other's hands together as soon as their feet were steady on the ground.

Vito barreled up to Enzo, grabbed him by the collar of his shirt and slammed him against the hood of the truck. "You were supposed to bring her to me immediately, not a day later!" he roared.

"I did!" Enzo fired back. "She's here! We needed time to say goodbye, that's all. Truly there was no disrespect ever intended. We needed to figure things out. We knew you would never give us an opportunity. There was no disrespect intended."

"Pop!" Laura cried, trying to intervene. "What are you doing? I had to do this. I had to know. I needed answers." She grabbed at Vito's arm and tried to pull him off Enzo.

Vito was furious, and Laura's cries fell on deaf ears. "Not when it was convenient for you!" he bellowed at Enzo. "Right away! Right away, damn it!" He slammed his fist into the hood of the truck.

Laura shoved herself between him and Enzo. "Haven't I been through enough?" she shrieked. "I came here for him, Pop! I needed to know. It's been so crazy. I had to do this for me, not to ever hurt you."

Vito looked at Laura, whose shocked face sent a new wave of panic through him. He looked at Enzo with renewed fury. "Did you touch my daughter?"

Enzo blanched, shaking his head profusely.

"Did you touch her?" Vito snarled again. "I swear to the Lord in Heaven, if you laid a hand on my daughter—"

"Pop!" Laura snapped. "Pop! Stop it!"

"Did you touch her?!" Vito demanded. "Did you touch her? Did you lay a hand on my baby?"

Laura managed to wrestle Vito's arm away from Enzo and pulled on him, hard. They stumbled away from the truck as Vito continued to shout at Enzo. Laura grabbed Vito's face and forced him to look at her.

Vito's eyes suddenly cleared at the look of anguish on Laura's face. His knees went weak, and he swept her up in a tight, desperate embrace, breaking into enormous, heaving sobs. The train chugged closer.

"My little girl. My baby girl. I'm sorry. I'm so, so sorry."

Laura tried to comfort him. "I'm fine, Pop."

"I should never have brought you here," he moaned. "I'm sorry. I'm so sorry!"

"Pop," Laura said.

The train howled into the station and sighed to a stop. The sound brought Vito to his senses. He put Laura down, wiped away his tears, and gathered their luggage. He stormed up to the door of their car and hurled their suitcases over the threshold, much to the surprise of the attendant.

Laura didn't move. She and Enzo stared at each other.

Vito looked over his shoulder as he loaded the last of the bags into the train. His eyes went wide when he saw the expression on Laura's face. "Oh, no," he breathed. "No, no, no, no, no. No, Laura."

Laura turned agonized eyes to him. "Pop, I . . ."

"Laura Baccaro," he ordered, struggling to keep his voice from cracking. "Get on the train."

Laura inched toward Enzo, her face ashen.

"Lulu," Vito snapped, exasperated, "we are not missing this train. Please, come home. The tickets are paid for. We cannot afford to delay. We will lose our money. I will not leave you here."

Laura wavered, but she moved neither toward the train nor toward Enzo.

"Sweetheart," Vito pleaded. "I haven't slept in days. Please . . ."

He went to her, scooping her up in a desperate embrace. She suppressed sobs, but refused to break her gaze from Enzo's face.

"Come on, Lulu," her father insisted. "It's time to go home."

He put her down and searched her face. Her gaze drifted from Enzo for only a moment, and she nodded. Satisfied, Vito walked hesitantly toward the train, his eyes locked on his daughter.

Laura went to Enzo. They stood in front of each other with fingers intertwined, their gazes locked. Laura's heart was aching for her father and for the man she had come to love.

"Aren't you going to ask me to stay?" she asked.

Enzo smiled sadly. He kissed Laura's forehead and wrapped his arms around her. She shuddered with a sob.

The train howled a warning.

Enzo took a step away from her, reluctantly releasing her hand. She clenched her jaw and turned to the train, tearing her gaze away. Vito stood waiting in the doorway, and he offered her his hand as she stepped inside.

As her foot left the ground, the train lurched forward, wheels screeching. Laura turned in the doorway to look at Enzo in alarm. As if unable to control himself, Enzo lunged forward to keep pace with the train, locking eyes with her again as the train slowly picked up speed.

As Enzo ran after her, the landscape seemed to change in Laura's eyes, as if she were dragging his imagination with her. Skyscrapers made of gnarled olive trees chased the train. Laura heard the whooshing of the heavy velvet curtains opening, and saw sidewalks spring up before her eyes, pennies gleaming in the cracks of the concrete.

She saw Enzo as an old man. He looked at her, and the light across his face changed from dawn to nighttime to midday. The trees in the distance sprouted letters instead of leaves.

The wind caught her hair and her dress, and she turned to look at Vito, her hair billowing behind her. It was dark inside the train, and Vito's face was obscured in the shadows. She looked back to Enzo again.

"Pop," she said. "I think this is my home now."

Horror dawned suddenly on Vito's face.

Laura took a deep breath, as if she were about to plunge into icy waters.

Both men yelled, aghast, "Laura!"

Laura launched herself from the moving train. She soared through the air for what seemed like an eternity, feeling weightless, safe, loved . . . and landed squarely in Enzo's arms.

He stumbled back from the force, but did not lose his footing. Laura buried her face in Enzo's chest, laughing and sobbing uncontrollably, emotion crashing in waves over her. She looked over her shoulder, as the train whisked a furious Vito away toward the horizon.

Enzo shook his head in wonder. Laura managed a weak smile, a bit bashful.

Then, as if they had no moments to spare, their lips met in an explosive kiss that tasted of relief, excitement, and vanished fear, and of two worlds intertwined, *per sempre.* This was everything they had ever dreamed of.

The kissing did not cease. They kissed again once they clambered into Enzo's truck, then in Enzo's garden, and days later in the ocean, on a walk, in the theater, and wherever they could steal moments alone.

All the while, a brilliant silver star on the horizon watched over them, dancing and singing.

Chapter Seventeen

$\mathcal{L}$aura folded the letter in half, noting the blotches of ink where her tears had fallen.

Enzo kissed her cheek with bittersweet sadness. "What did he say?" he asked.

She opened the letter again, but not to read it. Vito's letter was fresh in her mind. She told Enzo that her father had confessed an unwavering belief that Enzo was indeed an outstanding young man. During the search for her, while she had been kept hidden away by her crazy aunt, many had come forward to assure him how beloved Enzo was and how well respected and admired his family had become.

This news elicited a wide smile from Enzo, who settled into the chair beside her to hear more. She went on, telling Enzo that Vito had written that his intense anger at his sister-in-law's vile deed had propelled him into rage and irrationality. The rage had been brewing for what seemed a lifetime. He explained how painful the memory of her deeds had been, and how he had buried it all so far down that Laura could never have learned the truth from him if she'd pleaded for it.

He told her that he loved both her and Ana the same, never differentiating between them. God had brought his beautiful children into his life, and he would always show them the greatest love, as would Caterina. Over the years, he saw no point in mentioning the hurt or betrayal that had occurred when Ana was just a baby. The simple fact was that his three children were simply sisters and a brother, and he and Caterina were their parents—one family. He had believed that was all anyone needed to know. He expressed his regret that he had allowed Maria to repeat her betrayal once again, and said he was deeply sorry that Laura had been a pawn in Maria's game.

He went on to say that he understood how much she loved Enzo. He now saw that as soon as the plane had landed in Italy, she had become his. He regretted that he could not return to her in Partanna once he had arrived in Rome. He had been tempted to go back, but he made the hard choice to honor the decision Laura made when she leapt from the train. He was glad she had landed safely—exactly where it was clear she was meant to be.

He wished Laura and Enzo well and sent his blessing. He regretted that he and Laura's mother would not be at their wedding. He urged her and Enzo to relocate stateside as soon as possible, and when they did, he and Caterina would welcome them with open arms. He prayed they would see each other again soon.

He stressed that he needed her to promise to stay away from Alcamo. He once again apologized that his behavior did not represent Teresa well and was so sorry that being back there had brought out the worst of all possible traits in him. As far as he knew, Maria was not doing well and was still in the hospital. *Ah, what a shame,* he had written.

"Be well, my lovely girl," he had said, and then he signed off by telling her how much Salvatore missed her and was looking forward to meeting Enzo. Laura adored her baby brother and longed to be near him again.

In the crushing silence of Saint Catherina's Church a few days later, on November 20, 1948, Laura stood regally at the altar, staring into her beloved's eyes. With no thought to the onlookers, the pair exchanged whispered words of loyalty, fidelity, and everlasting love.

When the priest pronounced them man and wife, they hesitated a moment before leaning in cautiously for the kiss that would seal their fate, *per sempre.*

When their lips met, a swell of music only they could hear ripped open the silence. Ocean waves crashed, fireworks rang out, and birds flapped their wings in thunderous applause. They pulled back from each other, shocked to be met by silence when their lips separated. They gazed lovingly at each other, their ears buzzing. Finally, they were one. They kissed again—slowly, deliberately, happily—surrendering themselves to the tidal wave of love.

The celebration that followed was sedate, out of respect for Teresa. The couple sent silent thanks upward to the special woman who had brought them together as they each lit a candle in her memory. Laura yearned for the presence of her family members, but she felt incredibly loved by Enzo's family and was grateful for their care and support on this most special day of her life.

Within thirty days of her arrival in Italy, she found herself married to the man who had captured her heart from an ocean away.

⟨✦⟩

That evening, Enzo carried Laura over the threshold of the dimly lit room that had been merely his bedroom that morning and had now become theirs. The white fabric of Laura's wedding gown caught a beam of moonlight from the window, illuminating them both.

Enzo smiled slyly and produced a small radio he had hidden beneath his bed. Laura's eyes lit up, then dimmed almost immediately. "No singing. No dancing. Remember?"

Enzo smiled and switched on the radio. *All or Nothing at All* warbled out of the speaker, and Enzo pulled Laura into him. They danced slowly for a few moments, grinning from ear to ear. Then Laura leaned into Enzo for a slow, exploratory kiss that took his breath away.

When the kissing was done, Enzo poured each of them a glass of wine, which had been sent to them by Laura's Uncle Dominick. He had a small vineyard and produced a very succulent Cerraculo di Vittorio. Laura was growing more nervous by the minute, in anticipation of what was soon to come.

Enzo raised his glass. "To Teresa," he said.

The glasses clinked, and the newlyweds each took a sip of wine. Laura took a second, and then a third. Enzo smiled. He took the glass from her hand and suggested they prepare for bed.

"I'll just be a moment," Laura told him, trying to keep her voice calm, as she headed toward the bathroom.

Once in the bathroom, Laura paced back and forth, excited and terrified. A very anxious Laura peeped her head out and said to Enzo, "I think I need to have more wine. Please pass my glass."

He passed her a full glass through the door. She swallowed it down and began pacing again. Her dress whispered as she walked. After more than a few minutes had passed, Enzo tapped lightly on the door.

"Laura?"

"Yes?" she whispered through the crack in the door.

"Will you come out?"

"I . . . I . . ." she stammered.

"Come," he said, his voice gentle and kind. "Come be my wife."

Laura took a deep breath and opened the door. Enzo had removed his shirt, and she stared longingly at his bare chest. Hesitantly, she took his hand, and he led the way back to the bedroom.

The process of transforming from just a girl to a woman took a week to complete. Laura was terrified and hesitant, but the childlike Laura, who was filled with many doubts, never doubted that she loved Enzo.

The passion grew with each and every day, and Enzo displayed an unparalleled amount of patience. Laura had a great sense of humor about all of this and often made fun of herself and shared many laughs with Enzo regarding her sexual inexperience. After a week, they never looked back. Enzo was an attentive and loving husband, emotionally and in ways regarding intimacy.

❦

Days later, Enzo's boss, whom all of the Fellini men had worked for at some point in time, paid the Fellini family a surprise visit. Giovanni let out a squeal upon realizing who was at the door. The two men hugged, and Giovanni escorted him inside.

"I came to see Enzo and his new bride," Mr. Nicolo Asaro explained. "But first, allow me to congratulate you on raising such a fine young man. Your boy is loyal and hardworking. Truly, Giovanni, I would trust him with my own life."

Giovanni beamed with pride and let out another squeal that caught the young couple's attention. They came hurrying into the kitchen. Enzo grinned from ear to ear when he saw Mr. Asaro sitting at the table. Then he offered everything he had: coffee, biscuits, cake, bread, wine, and nuts.

With great pride, Enzo introduced his boss to Laura. The gentleman stood up and took her delicate hand in his.

"It is my honor," he said in English. "You could have not found a better man or family to acquaint yourself with."

Laura liked him immediately. The rest of the family joined the impromptu feast, and the food and wine made its rounds. The table became a flurry of activity and storytelling, as Mr. Asaro filled Laura's head with tales of Enzo's good character. Once everyone was pleasantly satiated, Mr. Asaro removed an envelope from his jacket pocket handed it to Enzo.

"Enzo," he said, "please take this as a token of my gratitude for all you have done for me throughout the years. I know how much you wanted to continue college, and I know that you chose to rise to the occasion when your family was in need. I also know you had many offers to make easy money. I believe you are the only young man in town who has not tried to steal from me. You always did—and continue to do—the right thing. You are a great testament to your grandfather Peter, your father Giovanni, your family, and this whole town—and now to your lovely wife—but mostly to the man you are and have become."

Enzo's strong admiration for this man and his gratitude for his kind words rendered him speechless.

"Open the envelope," Mr. Asaro instructed kindly.

Enzo did. Everyone around the table remained silent, waiting to know what gift Mr. Asaro had bestowed upon him.

Enzo was silent for a moment, and then he said, "Ten . . . ten thousand dollars?" He immediately handed the check back to Mr. Asaro. "Oh, Mr. Asaro, it is too much. I cannot accept this."

With a wave of his hand, the generous man replied, "Enzo, your good work and honest nature saved me much more than this. Use this gift to show your new wife around Italy and just enjoy each other. If there comes a time that I need you, I know you will be there for me."

Soon after, Enzo and Laura set out on a nine-month tour of Italy. Wherever they went, they stopped at churches to light a candle for Teresa. They visited the Aeolian Islands, the Greek colony of Magna Graecia in Agrigento, Messina, Catania, Taormina, and the Greek amphitheaters. They visited Mt. Etna, Monreale, the Temple of Apollo in Siracusa, and the Vatican. They lingered a while in Rome. They went on to Florence, Venice, and Capri. Lake Cuomo and the Amalfi coast stood out among their favorites. They went on to Malta, and enjoyed the beaches of Sicily where the weather was pleasantly in tune with their delight. They explored wine country and ate enough bread and olives to last a lifetime. They shopped the marketplaces and shared morning café at various bakeshops at every destination. They enjoyed wine tasting at vineyards all along the way.

Easy and gentle with Laura, Enzo was also protective of her in a way that made her heart soar. He taught her about the land, political corruption, and organized crime, as well as the terrain, history, and geography of Sicily. He gave her some insight into her Sicilian identity while sharing what it all meant to him.

She told him more about living in America, and they discussed the opportunities available to Americans. Despite not being an American, Enzo had much to add to this topic of conversation. Laura's new husband, she quickly realized, was quite knowledgeable on virtually any topic. She was completely enthralled by all she was learning from him and from their shared experiences.

Their evenings were spent perfecting their second languages and becoming more and more intimate—physically, emotionally, and spiritually—with every day that passed. They were laying the foundation for a life based on passion, admiration, respect, and more passion.

⊙✧⊙

Within ten months of their marriage, Enzo and Laura found themselves standing on the platform at the train station in Partanna with luggage in tow. They had grown so much as individuals and so much closer together. Earlier, they had parted ways with Peter, who had blessed their adventure to America and reminded them that Teresa would be along for the ride. Of this, they had no doubt. Peter embraced them, saying that he, too, like Teresa, would be with them. He hugged them tighter and longer than one would expect, but he knew this would be the last time he would ever see them.

Now, they were faced with the task of bidding farewell to Josephina, who was near hysterics but excited for her son and his wife, and Giovanni, who could not find it within himself to squeal at this time. Laura and Enzo would be sorely missed, but the Fellinis knew what a great adventure awaited the young lovers.

When the train pulled into the station, Enzo and Laura hugged Josephina and Giovanni one more time. Then they made their way up the steps onto the train.

Enzo looked back as his hometown fading in the distance, and Laura looked ahead toward their destination, excited to bring her mysterious Italian husband home to meet her friends and family. A few moments later, their eyes met. Enzo pulled her close for a kiss, and as their lips touched, they both realized that their true home would always be in each other's arms.

Chapter Eighteen

South Florida, USA—2008

"Home," Laura said aloud to the empty house. Without Enzo, she wasn't quite sure what home was anymore. With a sigh, she shuffled again through the stack of photos in an old shoebox, pulling out random memories.

The storefront of her father's shop, 1949

Standing outside the grocery store, Laura and Enzo gave each other a nervous kiss before venturing in to see Caterina, Vito, and Salvatore. Once inside, Enzo found himself warmly embraced by his new American family. They scheduled a game of bocce for later in the day; Ana and Vic happily joined them. Vito embraced Enzo and expressed his regret at having behaved so erratically. The two men agreed to never look back on their disagreement. The family quickly came to love Enzo. Salvatore and Ana were thrilled to have their sister back.

Vito and Caterina hosted a proper, formal wedding reception for Laura and Enzo, with music, dancing, and wine. They made a special toast in honor of Teresa.

Group shot of the Fellinis and Baccaros, 1953

Enzo's family arrived in America to make a new life. Happily reunited, Laura's and Enzo's families merged into one. Love was everywhere. Peter, Enzo's grandfather, did not come to America. They never saw him again.

Mr. Asaro moves to America, 1954

Enzo's old boss relocated to America, choosing to live close by the Fellinis and Baccaros. Enzo spent countless hours helping him build his new life and company. They remained lifelong friends. Enzo never forgot how Mr. Asaro had treated him—respecting him as a great man, not the struggling kid he had been. Asaro Partanna Sicilian Olive Oil came to be known as one of the best brands of olive oil money could buy. It is still available today, all over the world.

She and Enzo in front of their house with Gianni in his stroller, 1955

Laura, nineteen, and Enzo, twenty-six, were expecting their second child. Gianni, just two, stood beside the very pregnant Laura. She kissed Enzo as the sunlight shone down on their first home.

Laura, Enzo, Gianni, and James in their tiny living room, 1956

Laura and Enzo, feeling slightly haggard, observed their two small children creating mischief all around them. Enzo's Italian accent could still make Laura's heart skip a beat, but his English had improved tremendously, as had her Italian. Laura took great pride in his success, and they both took great comfort in their large, extended family.

The back patio of their new home, 1960

Enzo and Laura stood on their back patio of their new home on their twelfth anniversary. The couple kissed under the moonlight and did what they always did best: danced, laughed, and enjoyed one another.

The birth of a daughter three years earlier had completed all that was missing for them. Hardworking Enzo had provided a wonderful life for his family, always taking on extras hours to be sure they had every comfort. Enzo had built his own bocce court. Many happy hours were spent there.

Enzo and little Tessa embrace in this photo. Tessa has her father's eyes.

Enzo looking somewhat gaunt but happy, 1971

Enzo lay in a hospital bed while Laura clutched his hand. A cardiologist stood at the bedside to deliver the news that Enzo needed a new procedure to save his life. Laura wailed, and Enzo comforted her. He took her hands in his and kissed her, softly and gently, until she stopped crying.

The backyard garden, 1980

Enzo and Laura danced in the garden despite the heavy humidity. Enzo was covered in dirt, which made Laura smile. Enzo could make anything grow: gardenia, wisteria, berries, fruit, tomatoes—it was all here. The scent of lilacs dominated every season. Laura brought Enzo a glass of homemade lemonade.

A grown Tessa standing in front of the former Baccaro storefront, 1985

The Baccaro store came under new management, and Laura sobbed openly as Enzo attempted to kiss away her tears. Laura had brought her children here many times to learn their history and see where their family began.

50th wedding anniversary celebration, 1998

The backyard had been transformed into a beautiful venue for a surprise reception. James and Tessa embraced their parents as the couple prepared to renew their vows. With tears of happiness in their eyes, Enzo and Laura shared a kiss. This surprise had brought family together from New York, Italy, and California. Teresa's daughters made this special trip.

Enzo at the kitchen table, 2002

Laura wrestled with Enzo to get his oxygen mask over his mouth. *Stubborn man,* she thought to herself. Finally, Enzo acquiesced and allowed her to put it on. She kissed his forehead. His health had started to decline, but his spirit was as strong as ever.

Tessa sitting beside a very frail Enzo, 2004

Ambulance lights flashed through the windows, splashing across Enzo's pale body as it is strapped to a gurney. Tessa held his hand. Laura kissed him before the noise and lights were sucked out of the house, taking Enzo with them. Laura stood in the front room, alone and bewildered. Her children and grandchildren were grief-stricken.

A random receipt among the photos for new hurricane shutters, dated 2006

Enzo tried to prepare Laura for the imminent possibilities. He tried to cover every situation that Laura might face once he was gone. He prepared a list of tasks to accomplish before he "passed," to ensure Laura's future safety without him.

Still passionate about his beliefs, he called his grandchildren and daughter to his side.

"When I was young," he said to them, very seriously, "we were outside, we were with people, we worked, we played, and we learned all types of skills. I didn't have a TV, a phone, a computer, or an iPad. Mark my words: these devices are ruining the world and they will ruin you!

"We had people, we had each other, and we had respect for everyone we met. We had church, God, and family. Family is not what family needs to be; distance separates more than you realize. Remember my words, 'girl'!"

"Girl" was the nickname he'd use for his five granddaughters when he had them all near. His one grandson was lumped in the "girl" group name out of sheer simplicity for him at this point. These varied thoughts, memories, and life lessons seemed to come often and at random times as he reflected on his life and anticipated the future.

Laura and Enzo surrounded by their grandchildren, 2008

Enzo spoke with each of his grandchildren privately, sharing his wisdom, wishes, love, and final thoughts with these wonders of his life. He received a call from Teresa's daughter Rose with whom he had shared a close, lifelong friendship. "I have not seen Teresa since 1946," Enzo said. "I miss her. I think it is time for me to go and be with her."

In March 2008, Enzo had a stroke during dialysis. The stroke cost him his eyesight.

In early May, Enzo asked Tessa to buy him a Mother's Day card for Laura, since he could no longer drive or see. As Tessa filled it out for him, he instructed, "Please sign it, *'Per Sempre, Enzo'.*"

This would be the last card that Laura would receive from him.

On May 8, 2008, Enzo refused to continue dialysis.

On May 18, 2008, Enzo passed away.

Laura closed the shoebox. Rather than putting it back on the shelf in the closet, she left it there in the empty living room and headed to her bedroom, closing the door behind her. Faces smiled at her from every corner of the room, those photographs a beautiful testament to the last sixty years. She smiled back sadly, but a deep feeling of pride swelled within her for all that she and the man she loved had created throughout their lives together.

"Home," she said again. She would always miss her Enzo, but she knew that her beloved husband lived on in their children and grandchildren. Until she and Enzo were once again reunited, she would find home there, among those she dearly loved.

Feeling determined to carry on, she settled into bed and placed her head on the cold pillow. After a moment, she rolled over and looked at the photograph of Enzo on her night table. It was the one she had first spied in Teresa's apartment all those years ago, the photo that had started it all for her. She picked it up, looked deeply into Enzo's breathtaking eyes staring back at her, and kissed the photo tenderly. She placed it gingerly back on the night table and then turned off the bedside lamp. Absolute darkness enveloped her.

The year was 1948. It was early morning, but the room was still dark. As the sun began to rise, it shone through the window, illuminating the bare walls. Gradually, Laura's face caught the light, and she opened her eyes sleepily. She rolled over to Enzo, who slept on his back.

She smiled and scooted closer to him, sliding her arm across his bare chest and curling into him. She nestled her head on his chest, absentmindedly tapping her thumb on his arm in time with his heartbeat.

He breathed in deeply and sleepily opened his eyes. A smile formed on his lips. She propped herself up and leaned over him. They stared into each other's eyes for a long, charged moment. She dipped her head to kiss him gently. Then she looked at him again. He pushed her hair behind her ear.

Laura, quietly, almost mouthing the words, said, "Per sempre, Enzo?"

Enzo smiled and nodded slowly. "Per sempre, Laura."

Afterword

When a daughter loses the first true love of her life—her dad—any random moment can serve as a reminder of the loss. Tears, struggles, prayers, one-sided conversations, beloved memories, and the firsts of everything without him—all of this seems to go on in a never-ending cycle. Nothing stings quite like that first Christmas or that first birthday without his presence. Equally and perhaps even more difficult is seeing the pain on your mother's face when family milestones are celebrated without that special man at her side.

Some dreams might convince you your dad is still alive, bringing on a whole a new level of pain in the light of day. You may suddenly encounter his familiar scent or hear his voice in the strangest places. You know you need to get used to the new reality of that empty chair, the quieter house, the vacant car in the driveway . . . a pit grows in your gut when you allow yourself to think this is forever.

How can you accept that someone who played such a vital role in your life is gone forever, for good, never to be seen again? When you think you have mastered the pain of it all, a reminder comes in the tune of a song, a scene in a movie, or even an encounter with a stranger who reminds you of your dad.

This will throw you completely off course, but this is part of the process.

Every emotion, every sensation, every sight that reminds you of him is more glaring and pronounced. You imagine this loss is simply not survivable, and if this is how you feel, what must your mother be going through? The guilt you feel when a laugh escapes your lips—or even when, by surprise, you enjoy a night out—twists your heart. At first, you question how you can dare do this to your dad, the man who was by your side all throughout your life. None of it feels normal or appropriate.

In time, you will be shocked to learn that you can, somehow, survive. Unwittingly and perhaps unwillingly, you process it all in your own way and in your own time. And—if you are as lucky as I have been, if "luck" is what one can call it—somehow you will find a connection to your dad that reaches through space and time to let you know he will always be with you.

My copper consolation—that's what I call my father Lorenzo's reminder to me that, although he has passed, he is always watching over me. The pennies that have serendipitously come my way in droves in the years since his death make me smile and wonder. They continue to help me heal through my process of grieving. Each penny he places in my path is a gift, and I save each and every one. I have hundreds of these copper treasures. My father could never be forgotten, but he certainly was not willing to take the risk that he might be. He is a mighty force. In this book, through me, he has shared this great love story to be remembered . . . *per sempre.*

Poems by Rose Marino

Although Teresa is portrayed as a fictionalized version of herself in this book, she was a real person and her daughter, Rose, is one of the gifts Teresa left behind. Rose has kindly shared her poetry here, with permission, in memory of her beautiful mother.

Reflections

A tear shed today for time passed
A tear shed for the youth that is gone
A tear shed for the me of today
A tear shed for the tomorrow unknown.

A Poem by Lorenzo Indovinello

In cielo c'e in terra non c'e
Le ragazze non c'e l'hanno
Le fanciulle c'e ne hanno due
Michele c'e la di dietro
e Pietro non c'e la ne davante ne di dietro.

Dance, dance, you must
Dance in the fullest of life,
Dance in the winter of life,
Every turn, every beat, is yours
Yours alone, live it, to the fullest
It is your time to dance the dance of life!
Cherish it, care for it, grow with it,
In spirit, in wisdom, in loving ways.

Rose Reflection

Time is like the ocean waves;
It never stops moving.

Don't let sadness rob you of your today
or of your tomorrow.

Oh, song, that brings joy and ecstasy!
Dream of love, joy in my heart, of yesterday....
Today, the same song brings me to another mystery of life.
Sadness, loneliness, of the time gone that will
never come again.
Joy of yesterday, sadness of the moment past.
You, gone forever; the ever changing circle of life.

Author's Note

Soon after the passing of my father, I began to notice the frequent and intriguing occurrence of a penny in my path wherever I went. The pennies usually came one at a time, but sometimes in multiples if one of my children was accompanying me or if my mother was also along for the day. This coincidence became more consistent and apparent as time went on. Even if I simply thought of my dad, a penny would make an appearance. I'd spy one out of the corner of my eye, half-buried under rocks or some other object easily missed by others, but to me so easily visible.

I often have a premonition-like sense that very shortly a penny is about to appear. I *always* seem to spot these shiny copper reflections, almost as if divine magnetism is at play. These penny sightings and the acquiring of these tiny treasures always bring a smile to my face, easing me in times of sadness and elevating my mood even when I'm feeling good. Sometimes the pennies are accompanied by other signs too incredible to be coincidence. The numerous occurrences that have coincided with the timing, situation, and magical moments in which these pennies have appeared over these last seven years have offered me serious confirmation. Earlier on, I had examined and questioned that nagging doubt that this could possibly be real. After all, my father was *the* collector of pennies, which we only found out about after his death, and perhaps I was trying to find meaning in something that really was a simple coincidence.

Then, one summer day, while vacationing in Maine, I stopped at my favorite seaside chapel, St. Ann's, following my morning run, to light a candle for my father as I often do.

The beautiful old sea-washed stone building, ringed by amazing flower gardens and overlooking the ocean, is a perfect space for me to pause and reflect. That particular morning, it felt so peaceful and soothing. I found myself alone in the church, which was not surprising due to the hour. I felt safe talking to my dad there and, as I usually do, I simply asked him to keep sending me reminders of his presence.

Known for its magnificent stained-glass windows, St. Ann's uses little powered lighting during the day, and that morning the sun was sending incredible colorful beams of light throughout the sanctuary. As I finished my prayers and turned to leave, I was again pleased to see a glimmer in a dark corner under one of the entry benches in the vestibule where those sunbeams could not reach.

I retrieved the penny, embraced it, and kissed it. "Thank you, Dad," I said aloud. "Thank you, God."

"A penny from heaven for you?" came a voice from behind.

I jumped; I did not realize that the reverend, a large and impressive man with an enormous presence in the community, had walked in and witnessed my private ritual. I spun around, feeling a bit exposed. I paused for a moment to collect myself and then asked, "Father, is it possible, can it be? You might think I am crazy, but I am convinced the pennies I've been collecting are from my dad."

"No, my dear," he replied gently, "you aren't crazy." He gave me a warm smile. "Tell me, what is written on that penny?"

I studied the penny's face for a moment, feeling a chill rush up my spine, and my hair stood on end. I replied, "In God We Trust."

The reverend nodded, and I felt encouraged to continue. We spoke for quite some time before I left St. Ann's, feeling elated.

That night as I was reflecting on my day, I was flipping channels and stopped on *The Larry King Show*. He was interviewing a physic couple. I was not into that sort of "stuff," but something compelled me to continue watching.

Larry asked the couple, "So you are telling me that we really can communicate with the dead and they communicate with us?"

They responded, "Yes, absolutely. You have to be aware and open to the signs that they give us. And they do. It is *not* by chance or coincidence."

Larry asked for some examples, and they responded, "When a song plays, it is significant. You will find coins, a feather, or even a license plate can provide a meaningful message. You just have to be in tune to the things happening around you, to look, listen, and observe."

I was intrigued and thought about what had happened in the sweet little chapel that day. I saw this as further confirmation that the pennies were, indeed, messages from my father. I fell asleep with some comfort and woke up very early for my regular morning run along the beach. Halfway through my run, a car approached parallel, and seeming as if it were keeping pace with me, the car passed and circled three times. The license plate read I AM A PENNY. The late Enzo had many of his own favorite or famous quotes, and I will use this one, as it could not be more fitting: "I REST MY CASE."

As I ran alongside the ocean, I began reflecting on the last few months of my father's journey. He had been suffering for quite some time before a stroke had cost him his eyesight. After the stroke, I made it a point to spend time with him every day. He remained mentally sharp, but after a time of trying to carry on normally, he expressed he had had enough and that it was his time to go. Blindness and Enzo just did not work. He declined any further dialysis, which had been keeping him alive. The doctors gave him ten days at most without it. He passed away on the tenth day.

Torn apart by my dad's decision, yet striving to understand his reasoning, I had pleaded with him to reconsider this choice. But he had firmly insisted that this was the way it had to be. And, as she always did, my mom stood by my dad's decision, as much as it must have pained her to do so. Above all, my mother would *always* respect the wishes of the love of her life.

At one point early into his blindness, I had arrived at the hospital early, only to find him alone in his wheelchair in front of the sink, carelessly dressed, distraught, and so unaccustomed to his sightless life. He had been instructed to get himself cleaned and dressed over the intercom without assistance. He had no knowledge that anyone was present. I froze. I did not want to embarrass him, but was brought to my knees at the mere sight of my father not being able to get toothpaste on his toothbrush or to find the soap that was sitting just beside the unattainable faucet. His hands were shaky as he pleaded for some help. I quickly took control and preserved my dad's dignity.

Watching my beloved father go from such a strong man to a humbled weak and blind man broke my heart. I felt powerless and helpless—feelings that were so unfamiliar to me. I had wanted something more than the sadness I was experiencing out of my last days with my father. I am grateful that I decided to record our father-daughter farewell conversation and videotape some of our last moments together.

Our conversation was deep, lengthy, and beautiful. We both said what needed to be said. Among the many topics we covered, I had asked my dad, "How am I supposed to live without you? How did you do it when you lost your parents? Please tell me how."

My father's reply was instant, "Talk to God every day. Trust in God. . . In God we trust." This was his response to many things throughout my life, and he now told me to do this once again.

As I thought about this last conversation with my dad, I knew I had the proof I had been wishing for. All of those pennies from heaven and the miraculous events that sometimes surrounded their appearance were indeed real.

When I returned home from my run, I immediately retrieved my most valuable possession: my father's voice. I felt a strong pull that someone *up there* wanted me to take this one step further. I pressed play. After a moment, familiar voices—one of them mine—echoed from the speaker.

"Dad, tell me your best memories of your best days? I want to know it all."

His voice still steady, he replied, "All the days I spent with my children. . . . All the days I spent with my grandchildren and family. The day I met your mother."

Listening to this, I felt a knowing smile form on my face.

This is only a small part of my story and the amazing connection I have with my father. To this day, he still makes his presence known to me. For this, I am so thankful. However, the real story is not about me or my fortunate relationship with these pennies. This is only one facet. The real miracle is a most amazing love story, spanning two continents, enduring incredible hardships, and keeping a death-bed promise that brought two dynamic people together to create *per sempre.*

From the very early letters to my mother to the very last—for over sixty years—my father signed every one the same way: *Per Sempre, Enzo.* This alone was my inspiration to share their story. I know it well. And now, I feel blessed to have had the opportunity to share it with you.

Coincidences or Blessing from Above?

would like to share with you a few of the otherworldly events surrounding the pennies from heaven so that you, the reader, can fully see how incredibly magical this experience has been.

On several occasions, whenever I shopped in the store where my father, Enzo, had once worked, there would always be a penny on the ground next to my car door. It was *never* there upon leaving the car, but *always* there upon my return.

One day, a couple of years after my dad's death, my best friend, Lee, and I had lunch at an outdoor café. Lee began telling me that she had visited with a well-known psychic in New York City on her recent trip. But my chair was wobbling so much that I excused myself a moment, and I adjusted my chair on the uneven concrete by putting a matchbook under one of the legs. Since pennies were always obvious to me, I did notice that the ground around me was clear. There were no pennies to be seen. When I could give Lee my full attention once again, she excitedly told me the first thing the psychic asked her was, "What is with all the pennies I see around you and your friend?"

A few minutes later, two gentlemen approached our table and asked if we they could share the outdoor community table with us. We gladly agreed, and as I got up to shift my chair over to make room, keeping in mind my need for the matchbook, I looked down and four pennies suddenly appeared where I had just adjusted the leg of the chair. They had not been there before. This was confirmation to me that my dad was most certainly near.

On another occasion, upon leaving a store with my mom, my dad's favorite song—"My Way" by Frank Sinatra—just began playing at high volume on the street, and as I looked down at my feet, there were two shiny pennies. My mom and I just looked at each other and knew my dad was with us. Once the song was over, the sidewalk was silent once again. One song, two pennies, and that was it.

These are just a couple of the ways my dad uses pennies and "coincidences" to let us know he is always watching over us. Then, in 2013, he used a different tactic when his eldest granddaughter, Jennifer, became pregnant with her first child. This would be my dad's first great-grandchild. When Jennifer was around five months along, she decided to follow the trend and have a professional pregnancy shoot with her, her husband, and the belly carrying their new bundle of joy. She chose the photographer I had recommended.

The venue was a beautiful open field—a popular spot for such photo shoots. Weeks later, when Jennifer received her proofs, she called me in sheer amazement and forwarded one of the photos to me. My dad's profile—just to the left of her and her husband, Tim—appeared in the shot. The image distinctly reflected my dad's appearance. This was his way to show all of us that he was present for this special event, and we all got to see his face once again. TJ was born, and although he will never meet his great-grandfather, it is our hope that he will know that Enzo is always there for him, as he is for all of us.

We do not consider these events and others like them coincidences. In fact, they are very real to us. Some may believe, but I am sure many may disagree. But if you listen, if you dare to open your eyes and heart, you may see, feel, hear, or embrace the memory or presence of someone you loved, lost, and are still longing for. The comfort these events provide are indescribable and offer such hope. You just have to believe.

Acknowledgments

To Pat Iovelli, for your belief, unwavering support, and encouragement: Through this entire writing process, through every great up and down we've had since we were five, and through all adventures yet to come, you are the sister God brought into my life. I love you, and I am eternally grateful for you.

To Lori Konsker, the best cheerleader, enthusiast, and resource I could have ever asked for: I am forever thankful to you; you have been a most generous soul and friend who supported me in countless ways on this journey. Your support has been incredible. Thank you.

To Kim Girardi for all the selfless, generous support and encouragement given to me through the years. Your friendship has always been valued and a wonderful, positive blessing in my life. Thank you.

To Nancy Newman, I am so thankful for our paths crossing. One chance meeting turned out to be something we both never expected. Your support and friendship has been nothing but pure and amazing. Many thanks to you. Hugs and love, my sweet friend.

To Janet Stratt, Amy Botwinik, and Marcy Fox: My endless thanks for generously sharing your knowledge and resources so freely with me. Your selflessness, amazing support, and wholehearted willingness to help others reach their full potential and achieve their dreams have left a permanent impression on me. Girl Power!

To Gary Rosenberg and Carol Killman Rosenberg—the amazing Book Couple: Thank you for helping me create the dream. We did it! Thank you.

To Jeanine and Lori Corrao: How lucky I am to have the love, support, and generosity of your two beautiful souls. I am so blessed and so grateful, and I will never forget your belief in this book, in me, and in Enzo and Laura's love. I will never forget how easily you offered all of this to me!

Cheers to Ida and Tommy, *per sempre*. Ida's heart will never be forgotten.

To Nancy Montenes Grasso, I still vividly remember that day when your life was changed forever. Your Mom would be so proud of you and all you turned out to be. She is a precious part of this story. She will never be forgotten. You are just as special to us.

To Father Anthony Muldery, my rock for all seasons. Thank you and love to you always.

To Sal Varvaro: You were more than just my uncle; you were my friend, my confidant, and my partner in crime. At times, I relied on you as I would have my father and you were always there for me. I will miss you forever. You were ever present as I wrote this book and always will be. You left way too soon; I still needed you. Thank you for so many sweet memories and for your daughter, Vanessa, whose generous heart is almost as big as yours! We are two fatherless girls whose bond does not need words to know what the other is feeling. She has cared for your sister in ways that would make you very proud. Thank you, Vanessa Necolettos.

To Jim Pagano Senior, who silently passed away one sad day: I miss the man you were to me, both a father-in-law and an amazing friend. We shared so many wonderful moments, and your love and loyalty will never be forgotten. You were loved so very much and will remain so, *per sempre*.

To Jacqueline Argentis, the most amazing photographer I know and a friend with limitless talent: Thank you for your time and care, and for working with me until we both were beyond satisfied. You get it! It is about the message. I love your heart.

To Angela Villamonte: I couldn't have done it without you. Thank you for loving Laura and Enzo as much as I do. Every tear you shed meant the world to me.

To Rose Marino: How blessed I have been to have a glimpse of Teresa through you, her beautiful daughter. I will always hold such amazing memories of you in my heart. Your love and kindness mean the world to me. I love how much you loved my father. Thank you for sharing your memories with me. Words cannot describe how much all of it and you mean to me. You help keep these two beautiful souls alive.

To Caterina and Vincent Varvaro, Anna Guanaeri, and Josepina and Giovanni Fasitta. I wish there could have been more, but for what we had and what it all meant to me, thank you. You will never know what the love and lessons did for me. Bittersweet times left an indelible mark. As for that first car, I still remember how you made me feel. Thank you from the bottom of my heart. I miss you all.

To my husband, Jim; daughters, Jessica and Alexandra; and son, Nicholas: Your love and support while I have been holed up for the last few years provided me the opportunity to go deep into my heart to learn and explore more about my own history and the people I love dearly. I hope this book will be a gift you cherish for years to come, a story to pass on to your children when they want to learn about their family and Italian heritage. I was blessed to have had the opportunity to get to know my relatives intimately through this experience. Thank you all for your advice, time, patience, and opinions along the way. I love you all dearly and *per sempre*.

To all the wonderful, colorful, and sometimes crazy people in my life that I get to call family or friend: Thank you for all of it. You are all valued and loved.

About the Author

Born in New York into a proud Italian heritage, Roe Pagano made her first foray into professional writing with *Per Sempre Means Forever: A Legacy of Love,* which is based on the epic tale of how her parents met and married. Roe has owned and operated her own successful interior design firm for twenty-five years, and her creative passion has taken her from South Florida to many neighboring states and into the northeast. From residential homes as well as commercial properties, Roe is well versed in her field. She is a passionate student of architecture, design, business, and creative writing. She lives in South Florida with her husband and three children. You can reach Roe at roe@aniandoliver.com.

41765773R00126

Made in the USA
Charleston, SC
11 May 2015